Gar Garrigue, Sheila
c l The eternal spring of
     Mt Ito

DATE DUE			

THE ETERNAL SPRING OF MR. ITO

The ETERNAL SPRING OF

 MR. ITO

by Sheila Garrigue

BRADBURY PRESS   NEW YORK

Bradbury Press
An Affiliate of Macmillan, Inc.
866 Third Avenue, New York, N.Y. 10022
Collier Macmillan Canada, Inc.
Manufactured in the United States of America
2   4   6   8   10   9   7   5   3   1
The text of this book is set in 12 pt. Garamond.

Library of Congress Cataloging in Publication Data:
Garrigue, Sheila. The eternal spring of Mr. Ito.
Summary: The fate of a 200-year-old bonsai tree is decided
by a young girl and an old Japanese Canadian gardener who
resists being imprisoned in an internment camp after the
bombing of Pearl Harbor.
1. Children's stories, American. [1. Japanese—Canada—
Fiction.   2. Japanese—Canada—Evacuation and relocation,
1942-1945—Fiction.   3. Bonsai—Fiction.   4. Gardeners—
Fiction.]   I. Title.
PZ7.G1847Et   1985   [Fic]   85-5687
ISBN 0-02-737300-2

For my indomitable mother
KATHLEEN HAYES HOGG

1

October 15, 1941
Vancouver, British Columbia, Canada

Sara stared at the fifty-seventh page of her history book and all the lines seemed to run together. So many words about one man who'd lived hundreds of years ago. Who cared about boring old Jacques Cartier on a nice Saturday afternoon!

She slammed the book shut and wandered over to the window. It had been her favorite spot in the house ever since her arrival from England. The view was so peaceful from up here, so different from the air raids and search-lights and enemy submarines she'd left behind. When she'd first come, Canada had seemed like another world, with different food and different speech and different manners. But now, eighteen months later, it was England that seemed like another world, glimpsed in movie news-reels or newspaper headlines or fuzzily recalled through the lines of her mother's letters.

She leaned on the windowsill. Across the bay, Grouse Mountain bulked against the northern sky, a sprinkle of snow sugaring its upper slopes. To the right, the westering sun lit the twin peaks called the Lions, guarding the city of Vancouver at the end of English Bay. She could see the water if she stood on her tiptoes. On Saturdays, there were always sailboats out there, tacking back and forth between the north and south shores, and fishing boats heading home to Kitsilano, and the big ferry chugging west toward Vancouver Island. It was all so much more interesting than her history book!

Sara heard voices below. Uncle Duncan and Mr. Ito, the Japanese gardener, were walking slowly up the long path from the toolshed, Fearless, the Airedale, close behind as usual. They were a funny-looking pair—Uncle Duncan so big in his brown tweed jacket, Mr. Ito small as a gnome beside him. So different, but for one thing. They both walked with a limp. Uncle Duncan walked stiff-legged on the right side, where his wooden leg was. Mr. Ito dipped to the left, where his knee had been shot through. Just now, they were probably talking about where the new peach trees should be planted. But long ago in World War I, they'd been soldiers together in the 13th Cavalry, the Princess Pats. Looking at them side by side, Sara couldn't imagine how little Mr. Ito had ever managed to hoist her tall uncle onto his back and carry him through enemy gunfire to safety. But he had, and he'd saved her uncle's life, and he had a medal to show for it.

After the war, Mr. Ito had gone back to his farm in the valley but it was hard to work it with his injured knee, and his sons were too young to help. Instead, he'd begun doing the garden for Uncle Duncan—this was even before her cousin Mary had been born—and he'd been coming ever since.

Sara leaned out. "Hello!"

Her uncle looked up. "Hello there, Sara. Finished your homework?"

"For today, anyway," Sara said.

He waved his pipe. "Come down here then. Mr. Ito has something he wants to show you."

Sara grabbed her sweater and ran downstairs. When she got to the back door, her uncle had already gone into his study to sit down. His wooden leg hurt him in the colder weather. "One of life's little mysteries!" he'd answered with a wry smile when she'd asked him how a wooden leg could hurt at all.

Mr. Ito was waiting outside, his old felt hat in his hands. He bowed deeply. At first, Sara had been embarrassed to have Mr. Ito bow to her. But Aunt Jean said it made him comfortable to do so and now she was used to it.

"Hello, Mr. Ito. You wanted to see me?"

"*Hai!*" The gardener's black eyes sparkled. "I find, Miss Sara. It perfect for you. You come see?"

She pulled her sweater on. "What? What did you find?"

"You see. You see."

He hurried ahead of her down the path, his short bandy legs carrying him quick as a crab. The sun was still bright but there was a chill in the air.

Sara shivered a little. "Winter's coming, Mr. Ito."

"Winter every year come, Sara-*chan*. But spring every year come after."

She smiled. Mr. Ito never said much but whatever he said in his Japanese-English always sounded very wise.

They passed her sitting-rock, big and gray and smooth. Something long ago had hollowed it out in just the right way to form a comfortable lap. When it was empty, the hollow beckoned a welcome, and when she climbed into it, she felt a part of it. Together, they were complete.

Mr. Ito always nodded when he saw her there. "*Wah,*" he'd say, his face crinkling into a thousand lines. "Now rock happy, Sara-*chan*. You make harmony in my garden." So she often curled up on her sitting-rock to watch him as he bent over the plants, his gnarled fingers working among the stems and flowers like part of the growing thing.

Sometimes not a word was spoken. But sometimes he spoke of the Japan of his childhood, of the beautiful mountains and gardens there, of the gentle emperor who was the direct descendant of the Sun Goddess, Amaterasu, and of Shinto, the folk religion he'd grown up in, its shrines scattered through the countryside to honor the kami, or spirits, which controlled every aspect of their lives.

Sometimes, she'd pretend she was back in England,

watching her father instead of Mr. Ito, and she'd wonder if he'd had time to prune his roses. He'd always said you couldn't neglect the pruning, but these days he had to spend all his time up in his Spitfire fighter, heading off the German bombers. There wasn't much time for roses with a war on.

Mr. Ito had built a bench behind the toolshed. He called it his *engawa*. It was sturdily made of wood and ran the length of the little building, about three feet above the ground. An awning of wooden strips gave the plants on the *engawa* protection from heavy rain or burning sun.

Now Mr. Ito stopped beside it. "Winter come soon like you say, Sara-*chan*. Now is right time to start bonsai."

Sara had been wanting to try growing a bonsai for a long time. Mr. Ito had a collection of them standing on the *engawa*, tiny delicate trees perfect in every detail, growing in dishes so shallow there seemed no room at all for their roots.

"You've found something for me to make a bonsai with? Where? Oh, let me see, Mr. Ito!"

He grinned. "I have in toolshed." He ducked into the little building and brought out a mass of bare branches covered with twigs, all growing out of one heavy stem. At the base of the stem, three thick roots and many hairlike rootlets ran out in different directions through a clump of earth.

Sara stared. What Mr. Ito was holding didn't look the least bit like any of the plants on his bench. She didn't want to be rude, especially when he seemed so pleased, but she was disappointed. She didn't know what to say.

"Is . . . is that it, Mr. Ito?"

"Hai." He smiled. "This perfect for young girl. It flowering quince."

Sara touched it gingerly. How could she ever make this poor thing beautiful?

"You will work with it, Sara-*chan*. It bloom for you. You will see," Mr. Ito said.

"Sara! Sara, are you there?" Aunt Jean's plump figure appeared around the corner of the toolshed. "Oh, good afternoon, Mr. Ito. Sara, have you seen Jamie anywhere?"

Sara shook her head. Her cousin had been gone all afternoon. "Maybe he's taken the *Raider* out," she suggested.

"Well, he's in trouble if he did. He's supposed to tell someone whenever he takes out that boat. And he knows very well I wanted him to clean up his room today!"

Sara grinned.

Aunt Jean sighed. "Well, if you do see him, Sara, tell him to come in to me. I'm trying to get the house tidied up. Mary's bringing some servicemen home for dinner tonight and Jamie's room looks perfectly dreadful!" She turned to Mr. Ito. "Mr. Ito, would you bring one of the bonsai up to the house later on? I want to spruce up the living room." She pointed out one of the plants on the *engawa*. It was only twelve inches high, but in every way except height it was a complete and perfect

6

tree. She laughed. "I guess the best choice for 'sprucing up' the living room would be the Yeddo spruce!"

Mr. Ito bowed. "*Hai.* I bring before I go home, Missee Cameron."

"Thank you. And oh, Mr. Ito, while I think of it . . . would you be kind enough to tell Mrs. Ito that the alterations were very nicely done. And that I'd like to bring Sara and the other girls on Tuesday for a fitting on their bridesmaids' dresses."

Mr. Ito bowed. "Mrs. Ito happy her work satisfactory. Miss Mary's wedding pretty soon now. I remember her as so small flower bud. Now she ready to bloom."

Aunt Jean smiled. "Just a couple of months, Mr. Ito. Her fiancé is leaving the garrison in Hong Kong on the tenth of December. He'll get home just in time for a Christmas wedding." She gazed at the flower beds, full of crimson zinnias and yellow mums. "Everything's so lovely. I swear these flowers are actually happy to be here!"

Mr. Ito's weathered face wrinkled into a smile. He bowed and pointed to the tangle of branches on the *engawa*. "Now I teach Miss Sara make bonsai."

Aunt Jean looked doubtful. "With those?"

He laughed, his eyes bright. "You see. Is perfect for Miss Sara."

"Well, I think she's got her work cut out for her!" Aunt Jean turned back toward the house. "And I have mine cut out for me! I must get busy in the kitchen this minute. Sara, don't forget. If you see Jamie, send him straight inside!"

"I will."

2

Sara turned and wandered along the *engawa,* looking at the bonsai. There was a gnarled alder tree, its roots gripping the soil for dear life. Mr. Ito called it *fukinagashi,* because it looked as if a strong wind was trying to drag it away. Next to it, there was a group of seven tiny birches all in one dish, the *saikei,* their last clinging leaves shivering in the breeze off the bay. Then there was a little juniper, in *kengai* style, tumbling like a waterfall down over the pedestal it stood upon. Mr. Ito's patient fingers had made each of these tiny landscapes. And each existed in a shallow dish with only a few inches of soil in it to hold the bonsai steady and keep it alive.

"Which you liking best today, Sara-*chan?*"

It was a game they played. It depended on her mood. On days when she was swamped with homework and chores, she'd visit the birch bonsai. The tiny trees seemed to invite her in among them and she could imagine herself resting on the mossy ground beneath, looking up through the delicate pattern of leaves to the calm, calm sky.

Other days, when the news from the war was bad, she'd kneel in front of the *bonkei*. This was an entire miniature world in its little oblong dish—trees, rocks, grass, moss, plants, even a tiny wooden bridge over a stream made of carefully brushed sand. The *bonkei* world was such a peaceful place, always there, always the same, unchanging in a changing world.

"Which today, Sara-*chan*?"

"Today . . ." Sara walked to the other end. "Today . . . my favorite is the old beech tree." She touched it, running her fingers over the scaly bark, tracing the outline of the hollow at the base of its trunk. "This old beech looks as if it's been through a lot. And that's just the way I feel, after studying Jacques Cartier all afternoon!"

Mr. Ito smiled and picked up the branches on the bench. He held them out to her. "It late. We start quince bonsai before I go. First, you find shape. Shape of tree hides among branches."

"How can I tell?" Sara asked.

"Find harmony in tree. It must please you, Sara-*chan*. When you finish, you have chosen few branches out of many. Maybe five, maybe three. You choose branches which tell you of peace . . . or joy . . . or strength . . . or struggle . . . Let tree tell you. Look carefully. Listen to what tree says."

Sara studied the branches. "Well . . . there's a strong

9

branch here . . . and here . . . but I like the way this one points up and this one reaches out . . ."

"*Hai, hai!*" Mr. Ito beamed. "Very good."

"What happens now, Mr. Ito? Do I cut away all the other branches, so the shape shows up?"

"You learn well, Sara-*chan*. You hear what tree says to you. Now begin." He pulled clippers from his pocket.

Sara's hand trembled a little. She snipped at the extra branches until she was left with a three-pointed shape that seemed somehow right. She looked at her quince. Then at the alder and the beech. Then back at her quince.

"All these little twigs look untidy . . ."

"*Hai,*" said Mr. Ito.

One by one, Sara snipped off the twigs, then held the quince away, studying its outline against the sky. "It looks very bare!" She put it down in dismay. "I've done too much! I've ruined it!"

"No, Sara-*chan*. Is good. Roots would waste strength on too many twigs. Now they have more for what is left." He smiled. "So . . . now you have freed spirit of tree so it can speak. What it says to you?"

Sara laughed in relief. "It says 'Brr! I'm cold. Plant me quickly!'"

Mr. Ito ducked into the shed and brought out a gray-brown clay pot with two holes in its base.

They found some pebbles which they put in the bottom. Then Sara made a mixture of the different soils from the big barrels inside the shed and half filled the pot. Finally, she took the quince and placed it on top, spreading its roots and packing the earth round them tenderly, until the plant was supported. She backed away and looked at it. The little tree stood a bit to one side of the center of the pot, something she'd noticed all Mr. Ito's bonsai did. She hadn't been thinking about that when she'd planted hers. The roots had just placed themselves that way. It was as if this little plant had said to itself—I want to be a good bonsai tree and I'm going to help Sara make it happen. She smiled at her quince.

"Something's missing, though, Mr. Ito. Oh . . . I know . . . moss. It needs moss, like you have on the *bonkei*."

"Moss grow under apple tree." Mr. Ito pointed to the corner of the garden.

Soon there were several pieces of velvety moss tucked around the quince. And suddenly it looked as if it had been growing in the pot for years. Sara was satisfied.

"Shall I water it, Mr. Ito?"

"A little. Not much, Sara-*chan*. In winter, quince must rest. Must not grow. And it must sleep inside shed every night, in case frost come."

Sara dipped some water from the rain barrel and moistened the mossy blanket around the base of the little tree. It was like a christening. Then she picked up her bonsai and carried it in front of her into the shed. The bench inside was cluttered with tools and, at the other end, a dark shape took up much of the space.

"Wait, Sara-*chan*. I move this." Mr. Ito hurried ahead of her.

As her eyes got used to the gloom, Sara saw what it was. It was another bonsai, but different from any she had seen before. Squat, majestic, ancient, its ridged trunk rose up from a rock. Its roots were totally visible, spreading and curling around the edges of the rock. Looking at it, she couldn't tell for sure whether the rock held the tree or the tree held the rock. Locked together, they looked as if they were fighting each other. Or maybe loving each other. They were complete together. They could not exist apart.

Sara put her quince down and went closer. She stared at the strange bonsai. Something about it forbade her to touch it. "But . . . it's not growing in anything . . . I mean . . . there's no dirt . . . no dish . . . it's just growing on . . . the rock. How does it live?"

"Is wonder."

"I've never seen it here before."

"It belong family Ito."

"Did you bring it to show me?"

"*Hai.* And Major say I can keep it in shed for winter time. It like cold. It come from north. Ito's apartment too hot in winter."

"It looks very old, Mr. Ito."

"*Hai.* It with Ito family many generation. It come from Sendai in north Japan, where Ito family live. It grow on little islands there. Is special pine called *aiguro-matsu.*"

"*Ai-gu-ro-mat-su* . . . Why is it so special?"

"Is part black pine and part red pine. When Ito leave

Japan come Canada many year ago, father say me, 'Now you part Japanese, part Canadian, all same *aiguro-matsu* part black, part red pine. You and pine belong together, all same pine and rock belong together. I give pine to you so you can give it to your son and he to his. It spirit of your heritage.' So I bring pine from Sendai to Vancouver. And when I die, *aiguro-matsu* go to son George, first son, as is our custom."

"Your pine has come a long way from home . . . I wonder if my quince will go to England with me when the war is over. Maybe I'll be able to give it to *my* oldest child one day, just like your father."

"Sara-*chan* and her quince stay together long time, all same Ito and *aiguro-matsu*." His gentle voice was very sure.

A voice shrilled from the cliff path at the bottom of the garden. "Major Cameron! Sara!" The voice was frantic. " 'Elp! Is anybody there?"

It was Maggie Barker. "Sara!" As she ran toward them, her face was white.

"What? What's happened?"

"Jamie and Ernie! Oh, Sara! They're in trouble!"

3

She'd never seen Maggie look so frightened, not even when their ship had been fired on by German submarines on the way across the Atlantic. Maggie and Ernie, her brother, were spunky as the London sparrows they'd grown up with. But now Maggie's face was tear-stained, her brown freckles standing out starkly against her pale skin.

Sara grabbed her arm. "Trouble? Where? What's happened to them?"

"Oh, Sara, it's awful! Where's yer uncle? I've got to tell yer uncle!"

"Tell him what? Maggie! What's happened to them?"

"They're on the *Raider* and it's gone aground at the Point!"

"The Point!" Sara caught her breath. They were all constantly warned against going near Point Grey. Dangerous currents swirled near the base of the cliffs, where sharp rocks poked out of the shallows. Uncle Duncan knew someone who'd been pulled beneath the surface and out to sea in the twinkling of an eye and was never seen again. And the sands were said to suck down anything unwary enough to step on them. Quicksands they were called, because they gobbled you up so quickly.

Mr. Ito was already running up the path. "I tell Major!" he shouted over his shoulder.

"Where are they? I want to see!" Sara ran toward the cliff walk.

"You go on, Sara. I turned me ankle on the path and it's swelling somethink orful. I'll catch up."

As Sara dashed through the gate, Uncle Duncan and Mr. Ito ran out of the house and jumped into Mr. Ito's truck. "Sara!" her uncle shouted. "Jean's calling the Jericho Lifeboat Station. We're going to the beach!" The truck roared down the driveway, swerved into the road and sped down the hill.

Sara raced along the top of the cliff, with Maggie limping behind. The tall bushes on either side tore at their sweaters and scratched their legs. It was impossible to see through the thick foliage to the beach. They reached Maggie's garden gate and she paused, wondering if she should go in and tell her guardian, Mrs. Lloyd.

But Sara shook her head. "It'll take too long, Mag. And maybe they're all right. You don't want to worry her for nothing."

They ran on, stumbling over the pebbles that rolled

away from their flying feet. Suddenly the bushes ended and a gust of wind struck Sara in the face. She stopped for Maggie to catch up, her chest heaving, her breath rushing harshly through her throat.

The bay had emptied of sailboats—night was coming on. On the other side, hugging the north shore, a string of barges, their timber-laden decks barely rising above the waterline, worked its way toward Lions Gate Bridge. The Nanaimo ferry was just disappearing over the horizon. There wasn't a fishing boat in sight, all long ago returned to their moorings in Steveston or Kitsilano after their early morning start.

Sara's hair whipped across her eyes. The wind was freshening and it felt cold against her hot face. Maggie limped up to her. "Quick, Maggie. Let's go on!"

Maggie was not one to complain. She and Ernie, cockney kids from the slums of London, could take a lot. But her ankle was bulging hideously over the edge of her shoe. " 'Arf a mo, Sara!" she panted. She leaned on a big rock, all her weight on her good foot.

Sara leaned over the cliff. There were still a few people down on Spanish Banks Beach, watching the tide come in. She waved, shouting, "Some people need help at the Point!" They looked up and waved cheerfully back.

Below, Marine Drive wound between the bottom of the cliff and the beach and, as they looked down, they saw Mr. Ito's truck racing in the direction of Point Grey.

"Are you ready now, Mag?"

Maggie nodded and they hurried on.

16

The water, which had sparkled so merrily earlier in the day, had now turned black, except for little whitecaps running before the wind. Across the bay, the top of Grouse Mountain was covered with racing clouds. Sara looked to her left and caught her breath as she saw a dark squall line heading in from the west.

The path curved around, and suddenly they were above the Point. The cliff on their right fell away steeply and at its base the sand was littered with rocks. Sara crouched at the edge of the cliff. Maybe she could somehow slither down.

Maggie grabbed her shoulder. "You can't, Sara! The tide's coming in fast and there's no beach once it's all the way up."

Sara stood up slowly. "I know."

The *Raider* was caught between two rocks at the edge of the sand bar. Jamie was stretched out over the side, to keep the boat's hull away from the rocks, while Ernie was trying to scoop the water out of the bottom of the boat with his hands. How many times had Uncle Duncan told them to keep a baler in the boat! Ernie couldn't keep up with the water. The waves were breaking over the gunwales and the boat was filling fast. It wallowed and yawed at the mercy of the rising sea.

"They're in real danger!" Maggie cried. "That tide's coming in like a train, and if the *Raider* breaks up, the currents will drag them under!" Her voice was desperate. "I don't see 'ow anyone can get to them!"

It was true. They could see Mr. Ito's truck parked

back where the road ended. Uncle Duncan and Mr. Ito were standing helplessly at the base of the cliff, a half mile of quicksand between them and the *Raider*.

"When the tide comes in, they'll be able to swim to the cliff," Sara said.

"Not with them currents. And, anyway, Ernie can't swim. Neither of us can. Don't tell 'im I told you," Maggie whispered. "I know 'e oughter know 'ow at 'is age, but growing up in the middle of London, 'e never 'ad a chance to learn. Mrs. Lloyd wanted 'im to take lessons last summer but 'e wouldn't because the class was full of little kids."

Well. That was that. Jamie would never leave Ernie behind. So they'd have to stay with the boat, which was now thumping up and down on the hard sand as the waves hit it broadside. It wouldn't be long before it was in pieces.

Sara's heart was sinking. "Oh, where's the stupid lifeboat? Why doesn't it come?" She scanned the bay but the only sign of life was a trawler nosing its way around Lighthouse Point on the opposite side. Heading home from the Horseshoe Bay fishing grounds, it churned doggedly through the water toward Kitsilano.

The rain hit and the wind drove it into the girls' faces. It peppered the gravel at their feet like gunfire. There was no shelter on the cliff top, and in a minute their dresses were soaked through and their hair was plastered against their heads.

Suddenly, Maggie shouted. "That trawler! It's changing direction!"

They watched the trawler come about and begin to plow toward the *Raider*. As it pitched and bucked through the water, the faint sound of its horn was carried to them on the wind and its bow wave splashed high, a signal for the boys to cling to.

Sara's heart pounded. "They'll have to be careful or they'll go aground, too!"

It was as if the master of the boat had heard her. The trawler slowed and one of the crew threw out a sea anchor and then a man jumped into the sea and swam strongly toward the *Raider*, towing a rope behind him.

"Wot if the current gets 'im!" Maggie cried.

"It can't," Sara said. "He's got the rope around his waist. If he goes under, the people on the boat will pull him back." A smile was spreading through her.

The swimmer finally reached the crippled sailboat and pushed and pulled at it until he had freed it of the rocks. It bobbed free, bouncing like a cork. In another moment, Ernie had jumped over the side into the strong arms of the sailor and, with legs thrashing, was hauled toward the trawler.

Down below, Mr. Ito was talking excitedly to Uncle Duncan, gesturing at the fishing boat. The girls shouted down to them and Mr. Ito shouted something back, but his words were snatched away by the wind.

Out at the fishing boat, the sailor was pushing Ernie up its side into the arms of the crew. As soon as he was safely on deck, the man turned and swam back to Jamie.

Sara laughed. "He won't get Jamie to go without the *Raider*!" Jamie had worked on the *Raider* for three years, building it in the garage with bits of wood he'd found lying about in shipyards and on the beach, spending all his pocket money on rope and wax and nails. She was right. After a short conference, Jamie and the fisherman turned the *Raider* around and made the rope fast to its bow. With that done, the two swam slowly side by side to the trawler and wearily climbed aboard.

Just as they did so, the Jericho lifeboat roared around the Point.

"Finally!" Sara laughed.

The lifeboat came alongside the trawler to check that all was well, then pulled away, tooting its horn in congratulation. The fishing boat backed out of the dangerous shallows and, once in deeper water, set course again for Kitsilano, its blanket-clad passengers huddled in the well of the boat, the *Raider* bobbing along behind.

"Come on, Maggie," Sara said. "They're all right. Let's go and tell Aunt Jean." Sara helped her friend to her feet. "And you'd better put some ice on your ankle."

At home, Aunt Jean was sitting stiffly by the telephone, her hands clenched in her lap. In the hour just past, lines had etched themselves on her placid round face. Sara ran to her and hugged her hard.

"They're all right, Aunt Jean. They were rescued!"

"Oh, thank God! Thank God!" Aunt Jean began to cry.

"No need to cry now, Mrs. Cameron." Maggie patted her shoulder. "They're safe. A fishing boat picked them up. They should be 'ome soon."

"Thank God!" Aunt Jean said again. "Oh, thank God!" She shook her head, the tears running down her cheeks. "I've been so afraid. I've sat here by the telephone the whole time. But I swear if it had rung, I'd have been too scared to answer it!" She was laughing and crying all at once. She wiped the tears from her cheeks and blew her nose. "Well! I'd better get some hot tea ready for them. In fact, I think we could all do with a good cup of tea!" She bustled toward the stove. "And oh, good heavens! Mary will be home with those boys in uniform any minute and I'm not nearly ready!"

"I'll shell the peas, Aunt Jean. And set the table."

"Bless your heart, Sara. Maggie, whatever have you done to your ankle? Sit down, child, while I get some ice to put on it!"

Sara smiled. Aunt Jean was her old self again.

The kettle had just begun to boil when a car door slammed outside. Jamie and Ernie burst into the kitchen, still draped in the blankets the fishermen had given them, their wet hair slick against their heads. Aunt Jean hugged them wordlessly.

"It's all right, Mum." Jamie was grinning. "We're fine! I bet we could've got back without any trouble once the tide floated us free of those rocks. Still, it was lots of fun being on the fishing boat!"

His mother let him go. "You two are to go straight up and take a hot bath!" she commanded. "I don't want to hear another word until that's done and you're in some dry clothes. Jamie, you lend Ernie what he needs. And

21

then, my friend, you and I are going to have a little talk!"

Jamie's grin vanished. "Yes, Mum," he said, hastily leading Ernie from the room.

"I'll go 'ome and tell Mrs. Lloyd wot 'appened," Maggie said. "Ernie gives 'er fits with all 'e gets up to. She says she's sure she'll never get 'im back to our mum in one piece!"

Sara saw her friend to the door and went back to the kitchen. Aunt Jean had returned to her pie making and Uncle Duncan was standing by the table, packing tobacco into his pipe.

"All's well that ends well," he was saying. "We're very lucky not to have lost those boys. The most extraordinary thing, though, Jean. The fisherman who picked them up was Ito's son. It was George Ito's boat!"

Aunt Jean sank onto a chair. "Like father, like son," she said softly. "Our family has much to thank the Itos for."

"I know." He tamped the tobacco down. "Of course, I thanked him profusely. And I meant it from the bottom of my heart." He puffed furiously. "But wouldn't you know it would be a Jap fishing boat out so late in the day!"

Sara looked at her uncle in surprise. He sounded more angry than pleased.

"Oh, now, Duncan. We should be glad he was out there!"

"Well, I am. Of course. But those darned Japs work from dawn to dusk and then some!"

22

Aunt Jean glanced at Sara. "I don't see how you can fault him for working hard, Duncan. You're always delighted with the long day that Mr. Ito puts in."

"I know. But isn't it typical! You wouldn't catch a Canadian boat out that late. No wonder the other fishermen don't like the Japs. I tell you—there's no stopping them. Between the fishing and the farming, if we don't watch out, the Japs are going to take over around here!"

4

"The stars at night . . . are big and bright . . . deep in the heart of Texas . . ." Sara sang as she brought her bonsai out into the weak December sunshine. It was still quite bare, of course. It was silly to expect anything else in the middle of winter. But in a certain light, she thought she could just see a sort of bloom along the branches, a promise of life beneath the unpromising gray bark. She set it on the *engawa* out of the wind and tested the moss to be sure it had not dried out. It was cool and slightly damp to the touch. One by one she carried the other bonsai from the dim toolshed into the sunny day. At last, only the *aiguro-matsu* was left. She leaned against the toolshed bench, staring at it, trying to imagine anything living as long as this old pine had lived, strong and proud on its rocky base, its branches so serene above

24

its struggling roots. She dared not touch it. It was too royal, too mysterious. She'd leave it for Mr. Ito. He'd be coming to work soon.

She climbed onto the sitting-rock and, curling into its hollow, pulled out the letter that had come the day before from England. She'd already read it over and over, but here in the garden with nobody around, she was going to read it out loud and try to imagine it was her mother's voice saying the words—try to remember the sound of it across the many months since she'd last heard it, saying goodbye.

It scared her that it was getting harder and harder to remember her mother. She had a soft, light voice, Sara thought. Different from Aunt Jean's crisp no-nonsense tone. And she had always hummed a certain special little tune to herself as she cleaned up the kitchen after breakfast. Back last summer, Sara could still bring the tune to mind and sing it to herself. But now it was gone from her memory. She should have made sure to sing it every single day. She was nagged by the feeling that when she did finally forget what her mother looked like, that very day her mother would cease to exist. That's silly, she thought. Still, she closed her eyes tight for a moment, so she could picture her mother more clearly. Then she smoothed the letter over her knee, the paper cool against the palm of her hand.

It was dated September 3. Three months before, and six thousand miles away, beyond all of Canada and all of the Atlantic Ocean, her mother's hand had smoothed this same piece of paper, at her desk in the sitting room in Peterstone. Maybe Domino had been on her lap, boxing at the pen as it moved across the paper, his fur shining like black silk in the lamplight. Maybe Daddy had been home on leave, sprawled in his deep chair by the fire, trying to forget all the fighting up in the sky. Where had this letter been for three whole months? Uncle Duncan said she was lucky that it arrived at all, the way the German subs were sinking Allied shipping in the Atlantic.

The news the letter contained was old by now. But she wasn't really interested in the news. She just needed to know her mother hadn't forgotten about her, that she and Daddy talked about her sometimes and looked at old snapshots and remembered the time before the war when they were still together.

We miss you, the letter said. *We talk about you all the time, remembering how we'd have tea under the apple trees and laugh at Domino stalking rabbits in the kitchen garden. Today is September 3rd, two years to the day since war was declared. Nobody thought it would go on this long. But Hitler's troops have occupied all of Europe and much of North Africa and we simply cannot allow him to get away with it. Perhaps, now that Russia is fighting Germany, things will go better for us. It has already meant fewer air raids, I'm glad to say, but* ▓▓▓▓ *was hit the other day. Nobody can understand why. The German pilot must have thought he was aiming at* ▓▓▓▓▓▓▓. *He can't really have been targetting Mr. Boggin's barn! No harm done, though. Mr. Boggin planned to rebuild it anyway and the cows were out in the back pasture. But Domino's pal, the orange barn cat, was killed. Poor old Domino. He hates the sound of bombs. He runs to your room and hides under your bed.*

How tall you must be getting. I don't suppose we'd recognize you. Aunt Jean wrote she was getting you some new winter dresses. We wish we could see you. But when Mary and David Lloyd get married, Uncle Duncan hopes to get hold of some film and send us pictures of you in your bridesmaid's dress. We'll try to send you a picture soon, but of course ▮▮▮▮▮▮▮▮▮ *with a war on.*

Write and tell us about school. I wish we could talk in person. But the nice thing about letters is that you can read them again and again, as we do yours. We send you our love and a big hug and kiss. And Domino does too.

Love,
Mummy

Sara tried to stare through the blacked-out places in the letter but her eyes couldn't penetrate the censor's ink. Funny to think there was some stranger sitting in a musty office somewhere in England whose job it was to pore over other people's letters and decide if what had been written would help the enemy. Sara pictured a Nazi spy lurking in the shadows behind the Peterstone Post Office, waiting to steal her mother's letters for the vital information they contained.

"Ach so!" he'd mutter. "Ze Katz Domino no more liver has for his dinner to eat. Zis must mean ze war ze Chermans are vinning!"

Sara grinned, but her grin quickly faded as she realized that her mother's words, meant for her alone, might really be read by a German spy and had in fact already been read by the English censor. So the hands of a perfect stranger had smoothed this piece of blue paper and the eyes of a perfect stranger had read her mother's words, long before Sara got a chance to see them. Her mother had always said: "Letters are private and never to be read without the permission of the recipient." Well, nobody asked me my permission, Sara thought. The war's changed the rules.

The sound of Mr. Ito's truck interrupted her thoughts. Fearless barked a welcome, as Mr. Ito got a stepladder out of the back and carried it down to the toolshed.

"*Wah,*" he said. "You in garden early, Sara-*chan.*" His eyes brightened. "Ah. You take care of bonsai like good mother."

"I brought all of them out except the *aiguro-matsu.* That one sort of scares me. I'm afraid to touch it."

"It special, Sara-*chan.*"

"I don't know why it scares me. Perhaps it's because it's so old . . . I don't mean I think I'd break it—it's too strong for that . . . It's just . . ." She shook her head. "I don't know . . ." She followed him into the toolshed.

Mr. Ito smiled. "You have respect. That good, Sara-*chan.* You understand tree. And tree will tell you when you may touch it."

He lifted the ancient pine and carried it before him into the sunshine. As he walked the short distance to the *engawa*, he said, *"Namu Amida Butsu."* And, as he set the bonsai gently down, he said again, slowly and reverently, *"Namu Amida Butsu."*

Sara repeated it. *"Namu Amida Butsu."* It sounded like a prayer.

"That mean 'Homage to the Buddha Amida,' *Sara-chan.*"

"Why did you say it, Mr. Ito?"

"Ito always pray Lord Buddha in early morning, *Sara-chan.* And many time speak him during day. I offer him my work."

"Oh." Sara did not know quite what to say. "Maybe that's why your plants grow so well, Mr. Ito."

"Maybe."

"What are you going to do today, Mr. Ito?"

"Fix gutter on toolshed." He propped his ladder against the little building. "Cut dead branch off apple tree and chop for firewood. Check wires on young bonsai so not cutting bark. Take baby black pine from training pot and put him into pot more right for shape."

"Why do you have to move him?" Sara asked. It seemed natural to copy Mr. Ito in referring to the little black pine as a boy plant.

"Ito change soil. And look see what his roots are doing. If they grow too much, Ito cut back. He is healthy tree and, like all young things, he want go too fast."

"It seems too bad to cut his roots when he's doing so nicely." Sara shook her head.

"Ito living long time. Know better than pine what best. I do what must be done make him strong, *Sara-chan.* I train him up the way he must grow."

"That sounds like something our minister said in church last Sunday."

"Wah," said Mr. Ito. "Minister wise man."

"Sa-ra!" Her cousin Mary leaned out of an upstairs window. "Are you doing anything? Can you help me? I need you *desperately!*"

"Coming!" Sara called. "If I don't see you later, have a nice Sunday, Mr. Ito." Sunday was Mr. Ito's day off and he usually took Mrs. Ito to visit their second son, Henry, at his truck farm in Mission.

Mr. Ito bowed. "You, too, Sara-*chan.*"

Uncle Duncan and Aunt Jean were in the kitchen. Her uncle, still in his pajamas because it was Saturday, was reading aloud from the *Daily Province* while Aunt Jean chopped candied peel at the big wooden table.

Sara stopped to nibble. "I learned a prayer from Mr. Ito just now," she said.

"A prayer? On a Saturday morning? What next!" Uncle Duncan said.

"Well . . ." said Aunt Jean, "I suppose it's all right to pray on a Saturday . . . I mean, it doesn't really matter what day you say a prayer, does it?"

"Put that way, I suppose that's so. What was this prayer, then?"

"Namu Amida Butsu."

"He taught it to you in Japanese?"

"Yes."

"Fine thing. What does it mean, then?"

"It means 'Homage to the Buddha Amida.' "

"Well, I don't care for old Ito teaching you heathen prayers!" Uncle Duncan got very red in the face. "You'd think he'd have turned Christian after thirty years in

Canada. You know, Jean, I can't understand why the Japs don't assimilate better. They seem determined to hang on to all their old customs even though they're Canadians now. They should behave like Canadians instead of carrying on all these antiquated ways . . ."

"Such as playing the bagpipe on all occasions and eating haggis on holidays, like you Scots?" Aunt Jean asked calmly. "Really, Duncan, I don't see the harm in it. Why don't you go on reading me the paper?"

"Oh, all right. Well now." Uncle Duncan rattled his newspaper. "Let's see . . . Oh, listen to this. There was a bad fire at the herring camp on North Galiano Island last night—three taken to the hospital. What else? The Russians seem to be giving the Germans a run for their money. Oh, good Lord! That Mrs. McPherson over in Kerrisdale has had twin boys! How many does that make?"

"Nine." Aunt Jean poured the chopped peel into a big mixing bowl and got some walnuts out of the cupboard.

"I hear their oldest is in North Africa in the Tank Corps—nice boy, as I recall. Ambassador Nomura and his delegation are meeting Cordell Hull in Washington, talks going well . . . Good thing someone's discussing peace in this crazy world! . . . There was a tea at Mrs. John Turner's to plan the next debutante season and Mrs. Humphrey Jones helped pour . . ."

"What's a debutante season?" Sara asked.

"A lot of nonsense!" Aunt Jean sniffed.

". . . The Upper Fraser Fishermen's Association has given three and a quarter tons of salmon to Britain. Huh!

Trying to salve their consciences for cutting out the Canadian fishermen, I shouldn't wonder!"

"Oh, Duncan, really now! They're as Canadian as you are. And Mr. Ito's sons were born in Canada, which is more than you can say! I think it's very nice that they're sending Britain all that fish. I hear the British boats can't go out at all these days because of the German subs. Isn't George Ito involved with that association?"

"He's one of their bigwigs."

"Three and a quarter tons!" Sara tried to imagine it. "That must be millions of fish. Do you think they sent one fish for every person in England?" It was nice to picture her mother and father all the way over in Peterstone sitting down to a nice dinner of British Columbia salmon, pink and smooth, with Domino hovering hopefully in the background.

She picked a raisin out of the mixing bowl. "What are you making, Aunt Jean?"

"Christmas cakes. And no more raisins, young lady, or you'll not eat your lunch!"

A warm, sweet fragrance rose from the saucepans on the stove. "Are these Christmas cakes, too?" she asked.

"No, honey. Those are Christmas puddings. I'm making several extra to send down to the servicemen's canteen with Mary. They're nearly done."

"Do you think Sergeant Daly has gone overseas by now?" Sara asked. He was her favorite among the servicemen Mary had brought home to enjoy her mother's cooking.

Aunt Jean winked at Uncle Duncan. "Sergeant Daly . . . Now was he the farmer's son from Manitoba? Or the arithmetic teacher from New Brunswick?"

A blush crept up Sara's cheeks. "You know which one he was. He did those rope tricks. He came from Calgary and he said he was a real cowboy."

"Oh . . . Was he the one who promised to teach you to ride his strawberry roan? The one who nearly toppled my Royal Doulton figurine with his fancy tricks?" Aunt Jean smiled. "Nice boy. Reminded me of Mary's David." She stirred briskly. "And speaking of Mary, you'd better run up and give her a hand. She's been looking for you."

Sara was on the stairs when she heard a plaintive cry. She pushed her cousin's door open to find the room strewn with clothes, the bed unmade and Mary peering into her mirror at a tiny pimple on her chin. Her wedding dress hung from the picture rail, its brocaded train folded on a hanger and swathed in protective linen. Her veil rested on a hat stand on the windowsill. She'd let Sara try it on the day before, a cloud of gossamer tulle fountaining from a delicate floral headpiece.

"Oh, Sara!" she moaned. "Where have you been? I need you *desperately*!"

"Goodness! Where do you want me to start?"

"Could you roll up the curls at the back of my neck? And make the bed while I take a quick bath? I'll be grateful to you forever! I promised I'd take over in the canteen at eleven-thirty and I'm running terribly late."

"The puddings are nearly ready." Sara began brushing Mary's long silky hair before winding it around the rollers. Just one of Mary's strands felt thicker than her own whole head of hair. Aunt Jean said hers would grow thicker in time. "Can't grow in too many directions at once," she'd said a few days ago. "You're getting so tall, all your energy's going into that." Sara sighed. It would be lovely to have thick hair like Mary's. Maybe it would happen. One thing was certain. Silky hair was hard to wind around rollers. She frowned. "It keeps slipping out."

"Keep trying. It'll work in the end, Sara. I know it's hard. But practicing on mine will teach you how to roll up your own some day. You won't always be wearing braids. It won't be that long before you're getting all prettied up to go out with a boy!"

Sara laughed. She couldn't imagine going to all this trouble to go out with a boy. If he was anything like Jamie and Ernie, he wouldn't even notice.

Mary shook her head. "Look at this room!"

"Keep still," Sara said. "Why have you got your clothes all over the place?"

"I've been trying to figure out what to take on my honeymoon." Mary picked up David Lloyd's picture, which stood on her dressing table, placed carefully so that two reflections of David looked out of the mirror at her. "Oh, sweet, sweet David! Why won't you tell me where we're going?"

Sara laughed. "The bride isn't supposed to know. It's a secret."

Mary smiled. "I know. And I guess I also know we'll have to stay somewhere nearby, because David won't have very long before he has to return to duty. And anyway, with the war on, we can't go anywhere exotic. And all I *really* care about is being with him!" Her eyes shone. "Thank you, little sister. You've helped me think things out."

"Wait a minute! I'm not your little sister. And I haven't said a word!" Sara pushed some bobby pins into the last curler. "Do keep still or I can't do this!"

"All I know is that once you came in, my mind cleared. And you're just as good as a little sister. It's such a help having someone to talk things over with. Jamie isn't interested in anything but boats!" Mary twisted around in her chair and hugged Sara hard. "Oh, Sara, I'm so happy." Tears brimmed in her eyes. "I'm so lucky David Lloyd lived down the road and we met and I love him and he loves me. So lucky he's stationed in Hong Kong instead of North Africa where all the fighting is. So lucky he could get Christmas leave, so we could get married and have a little honeymoon . . ." She jumped out of her chair and danced Sara around the room, singing, "I don't want to set the world on fi-yuh . . . I just want to be-e . . . Wrapped up and warm . . . In Dave's arms . . ."

They whirled around and around till they collapsed dizzily on the bed. Sara stared up at the canopy above, her head swimming.

"I love your bed," she said. "It's so romantic to have

a four-poster with a canopy on top. In the book I'm reading, it says in the olden days they had curtains all around and you could draw them to keep out the drafts. I'd love that. It'd be like being inside an Arab tent in the desert . . ."

Mary sat up. "Well, little cousin, I've just had a thought. After David and I are married, we'll have our own big bed in our own little apartment. And I won't be needing this one anymore. So here's my wedding present to you. The day I get married, this bed is yours!"

5

 *December 7, 1941*

Sara pulled up the red knee socks that went with her plaid skirt, then put on her shoes, shining from Uncle Duncan's Sunday polishing.

"Hurry up, everyone!" Aunt Jean called from downstairs. "We leave for church in five minutes!"

Sara finished tying her laces, pulled a beret onto her head and put on her green tweed coat. She never liked wearing it because its scratchy surface made her arms itch, even through the lining, but it was her best coat and she had to wear it on Sundays.

Jamie and Mary were already in the hall. Mary looked very pretty in her pale gray coat, and she had a red pillbox hat perched on her piled-up hair, a veil wispy as a cloud shading her forehead. There was a glow about her, as though she were lit up inside.

Aunt Jean came through from the kitchen. "Jamie, go and change your socks at once!"

Sara grinned. Her cousin hated getting dressed up and usually managed to register some sort of protest. Today, he'd put on one red sock and one blue sock.

"And hurry up, young man. We can't be late today of all days."

"Is today special?" Sara asked.

"It most certainly is," said Aunt Jean. "Today the minister will read the banns for Mary's wedding."

"Why is he banning Mary's wedding?" Through Sara's mind flashed the image of her lovely pink bridesmaid's dress forlorn and unused in the closet, the wedding forever banned by the Reverend Mr. Colthorpe.

"Don't look so worried, honey." Aunt Jean laughed. "The church always does what is called proclaiming the banns for three Sundays before a wedding. It's simply an announcement that Mary Cameron and David Lloyd intend to marry and it gives people a chance to object."

"But why would anyone object?"

"Well, of course nobody would object to Mary and David getting married . . ." Aunt Jean broke off. "James Duncan Cameron! You go and take off those argyle socks this minute. If you're not standing in this hall in decent gray ones in two shakes of a lamb's tail, there'll be no Sunday dinner on your plate today!"

Uncle Duncan came in from outside. "Hop to it, young man, and give your mother no more aggravation!"

Sara stared. Her uncle was all dressed up. "Are you going to church, too?"

"I am." He adjusted his regimental striped tie. "I intend to sit with my daughter to hear her banns read." He hugged Mary to him. "After all, I shan't have her home much longer—she'll be a married woman in a month's time and away to her own little home." He kissed Mary on the forehead. "I'll miss my little girl."

I'll miss my little girl. Looking at Uncle Duncan with his arm around Mary, Sara suddenly ached for her own father so far away. She could still feel the rough surface of his Air Force blue uniform the day he'd kissed her goodbye. "I'll miss my little girl," he'd said. "But we'll be together again before long." How long?

"I've brought the car round," Uncle Duncan said.

"All right, let's go," Aunt Jean said, and they trooped out to the Buick. It was fun having Uncle Duncan with them. Most Sundays he stayed home and read the paper. Maybe today he'd enjoy church so much he'd go with them more often. But chances were his eyes would close and his head sink onto his chest before many minutes went by.

"I still don't understand why they call it a ban if they're not banning the wedding," Sara said.

"It's a different word, Sara—spelt with two *n*'s," said Uncle Duncan. Words were his hobby. "It comes from the Anglo-Saxon word *bannan*, meaning 'proclaim.' All it means is that the church is making a public announcement of the wedding. In the olden days, it gave the whole congregation a chance to anticipate and celebrate with the happy couple. And of course, it also gave anyone who wanted to, a chance to object if he had good reason—

39

if he, for instance, knew that one of the couple was married already, or that they were too closely related to marry."

He turned the Buick into the parking lot.

They had reached the church with several minutes to spare and everyone greeted Uncle Duncan as if he were the Prodigal Son. Maggie and Ernie were with Mr. and Mrs. Lloyd in the pew behind and, after low-voiced greetings, Ernie tugged Sara's braid. "Wot's the occasion? Why did yer uncle come to church?"

"The minister's reading the banns for Mary's wedding today," Sara whispered back.

Maggie's eyes shone. "Oh, 'ow romantic!"

"Ssh!" Mrs. Lloyd frowned at them. "Get your hymnals out and find the right page."

"See you afterward," hissed Ernie.

Sara liked church. She liked the feeling of belonging. She liked the smell of polish and candle wax. She liked seeing people in their Sunday best. She liked the stained-glass windows when the sun shone through them, making colored puddles on the floor. She liked reading the plaques in memory of dead parishioners and she liked the statue of the dead soldier lying in the lap of the Mother of Jesus. She especially liked the singing. But she didn't like the prayers. They seemed to be the same every week, and the Reverend Mr. Colthorpe didn't say them in a normal tone but used a funny singsong voice. It sounded as if he was showing off how well he could recite them while at the same time he was as bored by them as Sara was. There

40

were several all in a row and her knees hurt, pressing on the wooden kneeler. Sara had long ago stopped listening to the words, and she'd noticed that when Uncle Duncan did come to church, it was the prayers that sent him to sleep. He'd even snored once and Aunt Jean had accused him afterward of not really being asleep at all and snoring on purpose. The Reverend Mr. Colthorpe droned on about repentance. Why couldn't he say a nice short prayer like *Namu Amida Butsu?*

Sara shifted her knees and thought about the four-poster bed. She could still hardly believe Mary was giving it to her. "Don't be silly!" Mary had said, laughing. "Of course I'm giving it to you. There's no room for a four-poster in our little place. You can consider it yours." Sara sighed happily, picturing herself stretched out like a princess under the canopy, behind the bed's gauzy curtains. Actually, it didn't have curtains at the moment, but maybe for her birthday Aunt Jean would ask Mrs. Ito to make some.

"We shall now rise to sing hymn two ninety-six— 'Rock of Ages,' " said the Reverend Mr. Colthorpe. As they opened their hymnals, someone started shouting, right outside the church.

"Is that a newsboy?" Aunt Jean whispered. "He shouldn't do that in the middle of a service. Disturbing everybody! Someone should go out and stop him!"

Apparently one of the ushers agreed with her, because a tall man hurried down the aisle to the back of the church. As he opened the big door, the newsboy's words sounded loud and clear: ". . . attack Pearl Harbor. Extra, extra! Japanese planes attack Pearl Harbor. American ships sunk. Many feared dead. Extra, extra!"

Every head in the church swung around. Every face was momentarily frozen, eyes wide, mouth open. In the silence, the newsboy's cries echoed through the building and then, as the door swung closed, a buzz of voices filled the church.

Aunt Jean leaned across Sara. "Duncan, surely it's a huge mistake! Didn't the paper say the Japanese were having cordial talks in Washington?"

Uncle Duncan's face was an angry red. "They were, the blackguards!"

"Where's Pearl 'Arbor?" whispered Ernie.

"I don't know. I never heard of it," Sara replied, her voice shaking a little. She'd never seen Uncle Duncan look like that.

The Reverend Mr. Colthorpe called for silence. In a grave voice he announced that the hymn would be changed and that they should all rise to sing "Oh God Our Help in Ages Past." It was one of Sara's favorites. But this time the solemn melody rose toward the stone arches with desperate intensity and she could see tears glistening on people's cheeks. As soon as the hymn was over, many people hurried out of the church and the rest began talking again.

"Ssh!" Sara said. "Ssh!"

The Reverend Mr. Colthorpe was reading the banns for Mary's wedding. But nobody was listening.

6

The next day, nobody talked about anything but Pearl Harbor. At school, Miss Ferguson got out a map of the world and showed them where it was, on an island which was just a dot in the middle of the Pacific Ocean. Sara couldn't imagine why anyone would want to bomb such a place.

Later the children walked along the beach.

"Where did you say it was?" Jamie asked.

"In the Pacific Ocean," Sara said. "Hawaii. You know . . . where they do the hula-hula dance." She swayed her hips and waved her arms the way they did in the movies.

"Well, I don't get it," Ernie said. "Why are they bombing in the Pacific? The war's in the other direction."

"Don't be daft," Maggie said. "That's our war. This is a different one."

Ernie shook his head. "Wot gets me is they never said a dicky bird about 'aving it in for Pearl 'Arbor. Wot made 'em suddenly go and do somethink like this?"

"It can't have been all that sudden," Sara said. "Uncle Duncan says they must have been planning it for months. He's terribly angry."

"Well, of course he is," Jamie said. "It's not the sporting thing to do, is it? Attacking people without warning for no reason at all!"

"My teacher said they wanted to knock the American Navy out of the Pacific," Maggie said. "That way they could control the 'ole ocean, expand, take over all of Asia, like they tried to do in China."

Sara stared at the waves curling softly up the sand toward their feet. "How close is Pearl Harbor?"

"Cor!" Ernie looked solemn. "Maybe I was right the first time. Maybe this *is* our war."

They stopped walking and gazed out at the peaceful bay, the Victoria ferry chugging west, a small freighter heading for dock in the Burrard Inlet.

Ernie nodded at the freighter. "Wonder if 'e saw any Jap subs?"

Suddenly, Sara wanted to stop talking about the war. "I've got to go home," she said. "We're going to Mrs. Ito's at four-thirty for our last bridesmaid-dress fitting." She wanted to do something normal and forget about war, both the old one in England and this new one lapping at their feet.

Aunt Jean was waiting in the driveway.

"Good. You're back. Put Fearless indoors, honey."
Fearless liked to run after the car when they went somewhere without him. Aunt Jean called to an upper window. "Mary, we're ready to go. Did you phone the girls?"

Mary poked her head out the window. "They're ready any time, Mother. I'm coming right down."

They picked up Jennie on Alma and Caroline on Angus. Sara sat in front, listening to their chatter. Caroline was a former neighbor on Belmont and Jennie was a second cousin on Aunt Jean's side. They had all graduated from Crofton House School together.

The traffic was heavy when they got downtown and Aunt Jean threaded her way carefully between the trucks and streetcars toward Japantown. They parked on Powell and climbed the narrow staircase to Mrs. Ito's apartment above the Cho-Cho-San Restaurant.

Mrs. Ito greeted them with little bows and soft cries of welcome, hurrying behind them and between them and before them with tiny steps and fluttering hands, ushering them into her parlor. She made them sit down and brought rice cakes exquisitely arranged on a lacquer tray and small cups of scented tea, which they sipped while she went into the back room to get the dresses.

Sara looked around. There were family pictures on the mantel—George on his boat, Henry and his wife and three children standing in front of a tractor. On one wall there was a framed picture of King George VI and Queen Elizabeth in their coronation robes. On another wall hung a faded brown photograph of a man in a high collar and a woman in a black dress sitting stiffly on a sofa, staring unsmiling at the camera. Probably Mr. Ito's father and mother, who had sent their son across the sea to a strange land so many years ago. Had they ever seen him again?

A Canadian flag stood in one corner behind a little table holding a picture of Mr. Ito in his army uniform. Next to the picture, a small velvet easel held a medal pinned to a striped ribbon.

An old-fashioned sideboard faced Sara. Mrs. Ito had laid a snowy runner across its polished top and, in front of a statue of a fat Japanese man with his hair in a topknot, there were dishes of orange paste and brown liquid and a string of beads.

Aunt Jean saw the question in Sara's eyes.

"It's an altar to Buddha," she whispered. "I understand Mr. Ito turned from Shinto to Buddhism after the Great War."

"Oh, I know what to say," Sara said, nodding. *"Namu Amida Butsu."*

Jennie and Caroline stared at her.

"Wah!" Mrs. Ito came into the room, her arms loaded with yards of pink and green and blue net. "That good thing say, Miss Sara. Bring good luck!"

Caroline had a funny look on her face. "How come you know how to speak Japanese?"

Sara wished she'd kept her mouth shut.

Mary came to her rescue. "The blue dress for Jennie. Green for Caroline. And pink for little sister Sara." Mary

46

whirled the pink dress away from Mrs. Ito. "Put it on, Sara. Let's see how you look now it's finished."

A few minutes later, all three bridesmaids were arrayed in their dresses. They swirled around the room, swishing their skirts and singing "Here Comes the Bride!"

"Lovely!" said Aunt Jean. "You look like a bouquet of flowers. Now stand still and let Mrs. Ito adjust the hems. And I want you to try on your hats today."

As Mrs. Ito circled her on bended knees, Sara gazed at her reflection in the long mirror. Aunt Jean appeared behind her carrying a broad-brimmed hat with long pink ribons down the back, and placed it gently on her head.

"Oh! . . . Oh! . . ." Sara was enchanted. "But wait . . ." Quickly she pulled the rubber bands off the ends of her braids and shook her hair loose. It tumbled down her shoulders, wavy from the braiding. "There!" She looked like Scarlett O'Hara. She really did!

Suddenly, they heard the patter of feet racing up the stairs and the hurried scratch of a key in the lock.

"Mother! Are you all right?" a voice cried from the hall. Helen Ito rushed into the room. "Oh." She stopped short. "Oh, hello, Mrs. Cameron. I didn't know you were here." Her polite smile came and went. "Has anything happened here?"

"What thing?" Mrs. Ito got to her feet. "Why you home so early?"

"Have you had the radio on?"

"No. I do dresses for Missee Cameron." Mrs. Ito stared at her daughter.

"America and England have just declared war on Japan." Helen's voice shook. "I'm afraid, Mama. I don't know what it will mean for us."

Mrs. Ito sat down slowly. "Your father went last war. He too old now. Maybe George and Henry . . ." She shook her head. "How can farm work without farmer? Or fishing without fishermen?" She lifted her chin. "They go to army. They do duty."

"You don't understand, Mother." Helen sounded desperate. "Everyone thinks we support the Japanese in what they did . . ."

Coarse shouts sounded from the street below.

"Change back into your street clothes, girls," Aunt Jean said. "I think we'd better get on home."

In silence, they took off their pretty dresses and draped them over the chair.

"We'll keep in touch, Mrs. Ito. Let us know when the dresses are ready," said Aunt Jean.

"Hai, hai." Mrs. Ito nodded. "Maybe tomorrow. I work tonight. They beautiful, Missee Cameron. You see." She tried to smile. "Miss Mary looking so . . ."

A crash interrupted her. Helen screamed and the girls jumped backward as a rock hurtled through the window, sprinkling the carpet with glass.

"Good heavens!" Aunt Jean cried. "They must be mad! What do they think they're doing?"

"There's a crowd going up and down Powell breaking shop windows!" Helen said. Frightened tears stood in her eyes.

"Well, I'm going straight down to tell them what I think of them!"

"Don't, Mother! They might hurt you!" Mary grabbed her arm.

"They'll not hurt me!" Aunt Jean's eyes flashed. "I'll give those hooligans a piece of my mind! You girls come down as soon as you're ready!" She hurried out the door and down e stairs.

Sara ran to the window to watch.

"Get away from there, Sara!" Mary pulled her back. "You might get hit!" As she spoke, another stone flew through the window. It hit the flag in the corner, which fell across Mr. Ito's picture, shattering the glass in the little silver frame. The medal was knocked to the floor.

As the girls ran out the door, Sara glanced back. Mrs. Ito was on her knees, Mr. Ito's bright-ribboned medal clasped in her hands.

Out on the street, Aunt Jean was trying to talk to the crowd. "These are good people!" she shouted. "You're wrong to do this!"

"They've sure got you fooled, sister," answered a big red-haired man. "You'd better get out of Japtown or you'll be tarred with the same brush!" But he moved uneasily down the street, away from her.

They found the car quickly and drove out of Powell. A mounted policeman was at the intersection, stopping traffic from coming in.

"Do you know what they're doing down the street?" demanded Aunt Jean. "Those men are doing a lot of damage to a lot of innocent people!"

"Sounds just like Pearl Harbor to me, ma'am," said the Mountie. "Let 'em go ahead, I say—my brother-in-law's a sailor on the *Arizona*. God knows what's happened to him!" He turned his back on Powell and what was happening there.

It was a silent journey home. They dropped Jennie and Caroline after making subdued plans to talk the next day. Supper was quiet, too. Uncle Duncan was out at a Kiwanis meeting and nobody felt like talking.

As they cleared the table, the telephone rang.

"I'll get it," Mary said. She ran out to the hall. "Hello. Oh . . . hello, Mr. Lloyd."

There was a silence.

And then a scream.

And the scream rang inside Sara's head like something trapped. Rebounding and reverberating. Resounding and vibrating. Bouncing and ricocheting around and around the hollow of Sara's skull. Echoing and reechoing, until it was driven into every crevice and every cranny of her brain to lodge there, for ever and ever.

7

Mr. Lloyd came over later. Ernie was with him, standing close, fierce with sorrow. Maggie had stayed home with Mrs. Lloyd. The two families faced each other across the room like enemies. Sara thought how in ancient Greece messengers bringing bad news were killed. It had always seemed unfair to her before, but now she understood. She hated Mr. Lloyd for what he had come to tell them.

After that first terrible scream, Mary had withdrawn into a frightening icy calm.

"David is dead," she had said, in a high, thin voice. "No . . . no . . . I'm all right. I just want to be alone." And she'd walked into her room and quietly closed the door.

Shut out, Sara and Aunt Jean had hovered in the hall, listening to the silence. Then Aunt Jean had gone to phone Uncle Duncan while Sara stayed, crouched against the wall, waiting for Mary to need her, waiting for her to call out, "Sara, I need you desperately!" the way she always did. But no call came.

When Mr. Lloyd arrived, Mary came down. Her face looked old and chalk white, her eyes were open very wide, as if she'd decided that by stretching them to their limits, she could hold back the tears. It gave her an odd look of polite anticipation. She hugged Mr. Lloyd for a moment without saying anything and then separated herself from him, finding a seat on the sofa across the room. The family surrounded her, trying to brace her against what Mr. Lloyd was going to say.

He sat there, his face gray, his broad shoulders collapsed and bent, his big hands upturned and fingerwide as if begging for their forgiveness. His face had a helpless, beseeching look, apologizing for having to tell them of his son's death.

"I don't know much," he said, his voice rough with pain. "The War Department telephoned. They don't have the details yet themselves. Communications are all at sixes and sevens out there."

"Tell us what you can, Roger," Uncle Duncan said gently.

"Yes. Well . . . it seems . . . about five hours after the Japanese bombed Pearl Harbor, they did the same thing to Hong Kong. About fifty planes attacked the city and David's garrison was hit several times. David . . . David was on the parade ground with his platoon at the time. They had no warning. No chance to take cover . . . No chance to fight back . . ." His shoulders shook. Quickly, he put his hand over his eyes but Sara could see tears glinting through his fingers.

Mary, opposite him, sat erect, frozen. "It was quick, then?" she asked in a high, polite voice.

"Oh, yes. Very quick. That's what I understand . . ."

"I suppose, Mr. Lloyd, there's no chance at all that he survived? That maybe he's just very badly hurt, perhaps in the hospital? I mean, in all that confusion, there could have been a mistake. You know, he might be unconscious, unable to confirm his identity . . . There might be a chance of that, don't you think, Mr. Lloyd . . ."

"No chance, Mary." Mr. Lloyd raised his head from his hands and the tears ran down his face. "I'm so sorry, my dear."

Mary stood up. Pulled away from Sara's hand. Stood apart, dignified and alone.

"Well. Thank you for coming, Mr. Lloyd," she said. "I'll come and see Mrs. Lloyd tomorrow. Tell her how sorry I . . ." She gasped a little. "I think I'll go to bed now. I'm quite tired and there'll be a lot to do in the morning."

She walked from the room and no one dared go with her.

Early next day, Sara went down to the toolshed. She needed to do something ordinary. She brought out the bonsai one by one and arranged them on the *engawa*, testing their soil with her finger as Mr. Ito had taught her.

The bonsai stood serene as statues, gleaming in the morning sun. She knelt in front of each one, wanting to be inside the bonsai world instead of the one she lived in. When she got to the *bonkei,* she stared for a long time into the little landscape—the rocks, the trees, the bushes, the tiny plants, the wooden bridge and the stream made of brushed sand. The *bonkei* world knew nothing of bombers diving out of the sky to kill young men as they marched to a military band. It was a peaceful place frozen in time, forever safe from change. She gazed at her flowering quince, which like Mary and David's life together had barely had a chance to get started. Then she went into the shed to look at the *aiguro-matsu,* standing proud and alone like Mary last night, swaying against what threatened it, but holding fast. Hold fast—that's what it says, Sara thought.

She walked back to the house to get ready for school. Her homework wasn't done. She'd better read up on the habitants of French Canada before she got to class or Miss Ferguson would make her usual sarcastic remarks. She frowned in the sunlight, her head aching from lack of sleep. She'd spent the night listening to her aunt tiptoeing in and out of Mary's silent room, listening to her uncle's muffled inquiries each time she returned. It hadn't seemed right to go to sleep as usual on such a night.

Aunt Jean was moving quietly about the kitchen, trying to get breakfast without making a clatter.

"Mary went off to sleep about five," she whispered. Her own bright eyes were dull this morning. She looked closely at Sara. "You don't look too chipper yourself, Sara. How did you sleep?"

"Fine."

"You look tired. You'd better stay home with us today. I doubt you could concentrate on your work, anyway. Now sit down and eat something."

Sara sank down in relief. Jamie passed a piece of toast and she began buttering it. She was glad not to have to face all the questions and sympathy at school. She munched her toast automatically. It tasted like sawdust.

"Now, Duncan. What about you? Eat something. You look like a ghost!"

"Nothing to eat for me." Uncle Dunan poured his tea. "No!" He waved her away irritably. "Don't fuss, Jean."

Sara and Jamie kept quiet. Thick silence filled the kitchen, pressing down on them. Fearless put his head down on his paws, looking from one to the other without moving his head. Usually when he did that, they laughed to see his eyebrows going up and down. But today they didn't, and his eyes looked anxious. The pages of Uncle Duncan's *Daily Province* crackled in the quiet room.

"What does it say in the paper, Duncan?" Aunt Jean joined them at the table, perched ready to fly to Mary the instant she heard a sound.

"Not many details . . . They say it was forty-eight planes, five hours after Pearl Harbor. Forty-eight planes over that tiny island! They must have covered the sky! Mackenzie King says Japan wantonly and treacherously attacked British territory and Japan's actions are a threat to the defense and freedom of Canada."

"No wonder he declared war yesterday. I thought it was just in sympathy with the Americans. But of course by then he must have known about Hong Kong."

Sara shivered. All the time they'd been twirling around in Mrs. Ito's parlor, singing, laughing, beautiful in their bridesmaids' dresses, David had already been dead for a day.

Suddenly, Uncle Duncan pounded the table with his fist, so hard that his cup jumped in its saucer and tea splashed out on the clean white cloth.

"I feel so helpless, Jean!" He struck his wooden leg furiously. "My only daughter lies upstairs locked in grief, her fiancé killed in a war that hadn't even been honorably declared, and I sit here like a cripple, unable to comfort her or avenge him. At least you have the house and the children to tend to, meals to get, something to help us all go on. But what's the point of my going into court today when the whole world is a lawless mess!"

Aunt Jean put her arms around him. She didn't even mop up the cloth. "Ah, Duncan. I know how you feel. I know how you feel . . ." She held his hands in hers. "But the law's the point. The law against invasion and taking other people's property and killing. And the young people will go off to fight for that law, just as you did last time. But we older ones must enforce it here at home.

We can't let the enemy change what we think is important. If we did, they'd have won two victories instead of one."

Uncle Duncan shook his head. "I know you're right, Jean. That's what must happen in the long run. But this morning I want to go out and do battle and instead I sit here with the children, drinking tea!"

A truck pulled up in the driveway.

"It's Mr. Ito," Sara said.

Mr. Ito knocked at the back door. Across his arms, he carefully held the three bridesmaids' dresses. "Good morning, Missee Cameron," he said. "I have hats in truck." He smiled proudly. "Wife work all night. All hemmed, all pressed. Everything ready for wedding now, Missee Cameron."

"Everything but the bridegroom, Ito." Uncle Duncan pushed past Aunt Jean, who stood rooted in the doorway staring at the dresses. "That's one small detail that will be missing . . . Ito, you are to pack up your stuff and leave. I don't want you near this house again!" He wheeled and stumped away into his study.

Aunt Jean seemed to wake from a dream. "I'll take the dresses, Mr. Ito. I . . . I'm sorry. We have had some sad news . . ." Her voice trailed off. She bore the dresses away out of the room.

Jamie pushed past Mr. Ito. "Yes, Mr. Ito. We don't want any Japs hanging around here!" He ran down the driveway.

Mr. Ito stared at Sara.

"David Lloyd was killed on Sunday, Mr. Ito. In Hong Kong. Japanese planes came and bombed them, just the way they did at Pearl Harbor."

"Ai-eee!" His eyes filled with tears. "Miss Mary widow before she bride . . . ai-eee!"

"Yes. And my uncle is . . ."

Mr. Ito raised his eyes. *"Hai, hai,"* he said softly. "Ito understand."

He turned away. Slowly he walked down the path to the toolshed, his limp more awkward than usual. In a moment, he returned, the *aiguro-matsu* in his arms.

"This only thing I take, Sara-*chan.* I keeping safe for son George." He shook his head. "These terrible days and I pray Lord Buddha help us all."

"Is Mrs. Ito all right?" Sara asked, remembering the angry crowd the day before.

"She afraid, Sara-*chan.* She good woman, love Canada. We good citizen always . . . We not just born here— we choose come here. But yesterday our windows broken. And Mounties come to house of son George and take him away. He never do anything bad, Sara-*chan.* He good Canadian."

"Where did they take him?"

"Immigration Building. We not understanding. He born right here in Vancouver. He not immigrant. I think they asking questions because he is in fishermen's union. His wife crying very much."

Mr. Ito placed the *aiguro-matsu* carefully on the floor of the truck and climbed in. "I go, Sara-*chan.* Major-*san* angry now. Maybe after time go by, he let me come back." He touched her shoulder. "You taking care of bonsai, Sara-*chan*."

He put the truck into gear and drove away down the hill.

8

Up in her bedroom, Aunt Jean had laid out four big boxes. Mary's wedding dress with the long train lay on the bed, next to a tumble of green and blue and pink. Beside them were the headdress and gossamer veil.

"You can help me, Sara," Aunt Jean said. "I want to get these put away. Get the dark blue tissue paper from my store cupboard. It's on the second shelf—and mind you get the blue, not the white. Blue will keep the dresses from discoloring."

When Sara came back, they worked together, carefully packing tissue paper between the delicate layers of material, then wrapping and sealing and folding each dress into a separate box. Sara laid away her own and hated the Japs, knowing she'd never wear the lovely long pink dress nor the wide-brimmed hat with the satin ribbons. There'd be no pictures of her looking like Scarlett O'Hara to send home, no dancing with the handsome young ushers, no laughing scramble for the bride's bouquet, no slipping into her own canopy bed at the end of that wonderful day.

At last, only the wedding dress was left. It lay flat as a shed cocoon, the box beside it narrow as a coffin. As they began folding the dress, the phone rang downstairs.

"I'll get it." Aunt Jean hurried away to stop the strident ringing. Sara, poking tissue paper gently between the folds of the dress, did not hear the door open behind her.

"Was that the phone?" Mary's voice was slurry with sleep. Then, "Oh, no!" Her voice became a wail. "Oh, no!" She rushed across the room and caught the dress to her.

"I'm sorry! I'm sorry!" Sara cried. What was she doing wrong?

Mary sank to her knees beside the bed, cradling her wedding dress. Now at last the tears poured out of her. They brimmed from her eyes and ran down her face and fell on the beautiful brocaded bodice and the seed pearls around the sweetheart neckline and the elegant ruched sleeves.

Sara was horrified. "Mary, I'm sorry! I'm sorry! I didn't mean to make you cry!" She didn't know what to do.

Mary didn't answer. She just sat on the floor and rocked her dress as if it were a baby.

The family rushed in. Aunt Jean understood right away. "It's all right, Sara. It's good for her to cry. It wasn't natural, bottling it all up like that."

They all crowded around Mary, sitting on the floor with her. Even Fearless poked his damp nose anxiously at her leg.

"That's good, Mary. That's good, sweetheart," Aunt Jean soothed her. "Get it all out. You'll feel better."

"I don't want to feel better!" Mary cried. "I don't ever want to forget how I feel today—never, never, never!"

Sara could not sleep that night. She stared at the ceiling, her eyes gritty with exhaustion. Every time she closed them, she heard that thin, high scream—echoing, echoing. She got out of bed and went to the window.

A cold moon rode the sky over Grouse Mountain, cruel and aloof from the world it overlooked. Down in the garden the flower beds were blank of flowers, flat dark oblongs in the lawn. The twisted branches of the apple trees, black in the silvery light, looked evil. She shivered.

Suddenly she heard a noise. Out there in the stillness something was breaking. She peered into the darkness but could see nothing. Why wasn't Fearless barking?

Then she knew the answer. Fearless had cornered another fox in the toolshed. What a mess he'd made the last time, crashing through everything as he tried to catch his quarry. She could picture the fox, bright-eyed with fear, hiding behind the flowerpots, dodging among the garden tools—old Fearless knocking everything over as he went after him. Maybe it's the same fox, she thought. Fearless never caught anything. He was much too clumsy. It sounded as if he was making a mess of the toolshed.

Sara threw a coat over her nightdress and ran downstairs. The house was quiet. Slipping out the back door, she hurried along the path. Then she slowed. Fearless wasn't in the shed. He was on the path in front of her. Sitting quietly. Watching.

Watching Uncle Duncan, who had lined up the bonsai on the *engawa* like prisoners before a firing squad and now stood before them, a pile of stones at his feet.

Sara hid behind a tree, afraid to go any nearer. The cold moonlight had drained her uncle's face of color, but lit it as clearly as a searchlight beam. As she watched, he stooped for a stone, then fiercely, furiously and with soldierly accuracy, took aim. One by one, the stones shot from his hand, shattering the pots, splintering the branches. One by one, the bonsai crashed to the ground and lay in the dirt, all their grace and pride and beauty broken. When the *engawa* was bare, Uncle Duncan turned on his heel and limped back to the house.

Sara stayed by the tree, her heart hammering, until she was sure he wasn't coming out again. Then she slipped down the path to the shed.

The flowering quince lay under the *engawa*, its earthenware pot in jagged shards around it. She picked the plant up tenderly and examined it. Its roots, their protective soil knocked away, gleamed white in the moonlight. And from the main roots shimmered hairlike tendrils, new growth. Her quince had begun its journey.

"I'm not going to let you die," Sara vowed. "You're mine. He had no right to hurt you!"

Except for the broken pot and the shock it had suffered, the quince was not damaged. Her uncle's stone had struck the pot, not the plant, and the branches had survived the fall to the ground.

Sara carried it into the shed and found another pot. In the light of the moon streaming through the window, she put in drainage stones and then soil and tucked the flowering quince gently into its new home.

She hid the tree in the farthest corner of the shed.

9

 *March, 1942*

Nothing was ever said about the bonsai. When Sara went to the toolshed the next day, all traces of what had happened had been cleared away. Whether it was Uncle Duncan or Aunt Jean she never knew, but Aunt Jean did not suggest bringing a bonsai into the house again.

The winter weeks went by. There was a memorial service for David Lloyd the week before Christmas. After that, both households took refuge in their normal routine.

However, Sara stopped going to the Saturday morning movies, with all their shooting and screaming, and instead asked if Aunt Jean would teach her how to knit. Now they spent Saturday mornings in the kitchen, Aunt Jean working on khaki socks for the Red Cross, Sara knitting her father a birthday scarf. While they knitted, they sang Gilbert and Sullivan songs to Uncle Duncan's records. Sara's favorite had always been "Three Little

Maids from School Are We," but the record of *The Mikado* had mysteriously disappeared, so now she was learning the words to Jack Point's patter song in *The Yeomen of the Guard*.

Mary had always liked singing but she didn't join them. These days she slept late on Saturdays. She'd given up going to the servicemen's canteen and taken a job downtown, and by the weekend, she was pretty tired out.

Uncle Duncan didn't sing with them either, even though the records were his. Grim and unsmiling, he spent most of his time shut up in his study.

At the Lloyds' it was the same. In each house, the lifelessness and quiet pressed upon the children and drove them out of doors, and even though the cold rain slanted down almost every day, Sara and Jamie would throw on their wet-weather gear and tramp along to the Lloyds' after school to get Ernie and Maggie.

"I know 'ow to tell a Jap from a Chink," boasted Ernie as they leaned into the wind at the base of the cliffs.

"They look the same to me," Jamie said. "How do you know?"

"I read it in the paper." Ernie looked serious. "It's important to know, so you can spot a spy when you see 'im."

"Every Jap isn't a spy," Sara said. "Mr. Ito isn't a spy. He's a Canadian and he was in the Great War with Uncle Duncan."

"Then 'e's the best kind to be a spy, ain't 'e?" Ernie

66

looked around triumphantly. "Nobody would ever suspect 'im, would they?"

"No-o . . . but he isn't, so it's not fair to go around saying he is."

"What do you know, Sara?" Jamie commented. "Dad got rid of him, didn't he? Maybe that's why."

Sara shook her head stubbornly.

"Well, does anybody want to know 'ow you can tell a Jap from a Chink or not?" Ernie asked.

"I do," Jamie said. "Even if some people don't."

"Right then. 'Ere's the way you do it. Look."

Ernie hunkered down near the sea's edge. He drew two ovals in the damp sand.

"Now . . . these 'ere are their faces. First orff, the shape of their faces is different, see. Yer Jap 'as a wide face with big round cheekbones. Yer Chink 'as a long, narrer face with 'igh cheekbones."

Maggie frowned. "That's 'ard to see unless they're standing side by side in front of you," she pointed out. "And I bet there are Japs with thin faces and Chinamen with fat faces and then where are you?"

"Don't ask silly questions, Mag. I'm just telling you wot I read in the bloomin' paper."

Maggie fell silent.

"Now . . . the next tip-orff is the old mince pies."

"The what?" Jamie asked.

"Mince pies . . . eyes."

"Oh . . . yes . . . What's cockney for face?"

"Boat race . . . Chevy Chase . . . that ain't important. Don't keep interrupting."

"Sorry."

"Now, the thing about the eyes is . . . yer Japs don't 'ave no eyelids."

Sara couldn't stand it. "They do so!" she protested.

"Well, I know they 'ave eyelids. But wot I mean to say is, their eyelids 'ave a sort of fold over 'em, so they slant down smooth like."

"And the Chinese?" Maggie squinted at his drawing.

Ernie stood up. "Well, yer Chinese 'as more of a straight or upward slanting eyelid . . . And then, though they both 'ave yellowish skin, the Jap's is a bit more brown, like, and 'e can also 'ave rosy cheeks sometimes, wot yer Chinaman never does."

"I never saw Mr. Ito with rosy cheeks," Sara said.

"What else?" Jamie asked.

"I think that does it . . . No, wait an old cock linnet . . . Japs 'ave 'eavy beards and Chinks 'ave light beards."

"I once saw a Chinaman with a beard," Jamie said. "Come to think of it, it was sort of wispy looking."

"There you are, then." Ernie looked satisfied. "So now you know wot to look for."

"Well, I think it's all silly," Sara said.

"Maybe it is, maybe it ain't," Ernie said darkly. "You never know. All I know is I'm going to keep me old minces open."

"Anyone 'oo really wants to know wot a person is, only 'as to ask to see 'is registration card," Maggie said. "All the Japs 'ad to register right after Pearl 'Arbor. Mr. Lloyd told me."

"It isn't so silly, Sara," Jamie said. "They were saying at school that there are Jap subs off the coast. They sank a tanker called the *Emilio* somewhere near California. They could easily sneak ashore at night and pass themselves off as Japanese-Canadians."

"But what good would that do them?" Sara answered. "Uncle Duncan said all Japanese men except the old ones had been sent at least a hundred miles east of the coast."

"You're right," Jamie acknowledged. "A Japanese man walking around Vancouver now would stick out like a sore thumb."

"*Except* if 'e tried to pass 'isself orff as a Chinaman!" Ernie looked around in triumph. "Which only goes to prove you want to be able to tell the difference." He sighed. "I can't wait to join the army," he said. "I just 'ope the war goes on long enough. I want to be a commando like me old man. 'E 'as to go be'ind enemy lines with black all over 'is face so 'e won't show up in the dark, like. 'E's a master of disguise—'e told me 'ow 'e does it in 'is letters. 'E goes orff on secret missions. It don't 'arf sound exciting! Once 'e 'ad to pretend to be an Arab and ride a camel. Cor!" He sailed a stone as hard as he could into the cold water of the bay.

Sara watched it splash and sink out of sight. Would it hit a Jap sub lurking beneath the surface, waiting for nightfall?

"What's the time?" she asked. "I got a letter yesterday and I want to answer it before supper."

"It's getting late," Maggie said. "We should go 'ome, too. We'll walk with you."

The friends turned back along the beach and scrambled up the sandy cliff, using the hand and footholds they'd used a hundred times before. They'd worn a sort of path up to the cliff walk and Jamie had performed a ceremony one day last summer, naming it the Limey Path in honor of the English three.

At home, Aunt Jean and some ladies were in the living room playing cards. The children ducked past the door so they wouldn't have to go in and be polite.

"I'm going to sand down the *Raider*," Jamie whispered. "You can help me if you like."

Sara knew she couldn't expect rides in the boat next summer if she didn't do some of the work now. But this time she had a good excuse. "I will tomorrow, Jamie, honest. But right now I want to write my letter."

She ran upstairs and got a writing pad out of the desk by the window. As she filled her pen with ink, she glanced outside. The heavy clouds were breaking up and a gleam of sun glistened on the trees below. Grabbing a towel to sit on, she ran downstairs. Her sitting-rock was waiting. She spread the towel over its wet surface, then turned into the toolshed to check her flowering quince.

She kept it on the windowsill in the daytime but hid it every evening before her uncle came home. Almost three months had gone by since she'd rescued it from beneath the *engawa*. It stood there bravely, its bare branches elegant against the cobwebby window. She lifted it down.

"It's a shame to have to hide you," she whispered, pushing it carefully into the shadows.

She climbed onto the sitting-rock, easing back into its comfortable hollow.

It's nice here in the garden, she wrote. *I saw some snowdrops under the lilac bush. I think that means spring is almost here. Is it spring in Peterstone yet?"*

She stared out at the garden, missing the sight of Mr. Ito bending over the flower beds. It didn't really seem like spring without him. Would Uncle Duncan ever change his mind and let Mr. Ito come back? She looked up toward the house, where the ladies were beginning to leave. It would soon be time to help with supper. She bent to her letter, trying to imagine her mother and father here in the garden with her, the way they used to sit on summer evenings in Peterstone, their comfortable talk disconnected and lazy as the bees droning in the honey-suckle. That scene was becoming more and more dream-like, but she could still picture the garden. Better than she could the faces of her parents.

Supper was already on the table when Uncle Duncan came home.

"What made you so late, Duncan?" Aunt Jean asked. "I put the shepherd's pie back in the oven. I hope it hasn't dried out."

Uncle Duncan stumped around the table and gave her a big hug. "Sorry, Jeannie. It's been a busy day." He sat down and beamed at everyone while she filled his plate. "I'm pleased to announce that at last I am to be of some use in this war," he said. "They've asked this old peg leg to be on the advisory board of the British Columbia Security Commission. What do you think of that?"

"Oh, Duncan! Congratulations!" Aunt Jean kissed him as she put down his plate. "And they're lucky to get you! You can certainly be of great help to them with all your military experience and your legal knowledge." She motioned to Jamie. "Another helping, Jamie? Mary, some more? Sara?"

Jamie passed up his plate. "What do you have to do, Dad?"

"It's mainly organization, son."

"Thanks, Mum . . . Organization?"

"Yes. Anything to do with the security of the area. We have to plan in case of invasion, arrange for bomb shelters, work out evacuation routes, that sort of thing. Someone has to be responsible for the safety of the general population in case of attack."

"Is there going to be an attack?" Sara asked.

"Oh, I don't think so," Uncle Duncan said. "But we should be ready, in case."

"What were you planning today?"

Jamie frowned at her. "Maybe it's hush-hush."

"That's all right, Jamie. It'll be in the paper in the morning," Uncle Duncan said. "Mmm! This pie is good, Jean! I married the best cook in the world!"

"Oh, now . . . Shepherd's pie is easy." Aunt Jean smiled as she protested. In fact, everyone was smiling. It was so long since Uncle Duncan had been in a good mood.

He sat back in his chair. "Well, as you know, all Japanese men between the ages of eighteen and forty have already been shipped out. Today, we received authorization from Ottawa to ship the rest of them. Everyone of Japanese background is to go, every man jack of 'em."

"Good heavens!" said Aunt Jean. "There are thousands in Vancouver alone. You don't mean all of them? Not the Canadians?"

He nodded. "The whole bunch, Canadian-born or not, citizens or not. It's the only way. We've got to act quickly. It's for their own good as much as anything else. Ugly feeling is building more and more every day, with the bad news from Singapore and Burma."

"Well, Duncan. That's a big job! No wonder they need your help!"

Mary got up from the table abruptly and started out of the room. "The sooner they're gone the better!" Her voice was shrill. "They're barbarians! Heathens! I can't stand the sight of any one of them!"

Aunt Jean looked anxiously after her. "Where will they be sent, Duncan?"

"We're getting camps ready—up in the mountains. There are places up through there that have been virtually ghost towns since the mining petered out. It will keep them properly isolated. And it might even help the towns revive a bit to have a bunch of new people arrive. The inmates will need food, clothing, that sort of thing— it'll help the local shopkeepers."

It's not fair, Sara thought. They haven't done anything. What had Mrs. Ito done to deserve this? Mrs. Ito, so proud of her husband's medal, who had the king's picture on her wall. She thought about Hansi Schneider at school. His family was German but they weren't being sent away.

"What will they do all day?" she asked.

"Oh, they'll have plenty to do to get settled in, get the work of the camp organized. The women will do what they always do, I suppose—cook, clean, look after the children. The elderly people can help, maybe grow vegetables, that sort of thing."

"Suppose they don't want to go?"

"They must go. It's the law. That's all there is to it. Their people went to war on us and they must suffer the consequences." Her uncle sat back. "If there's more shepherd's pie, I'll have another small helping, Jean."

Sara stared at her plate. She thought about Mr. and Mrs. Ito finding out the next day that they had to go to a camp. She hadn't much liked the camp she had gone to last summer. It had been a lot of hard work pumping water to wash with and trying to light a fire with wood all wet from the rain. And the cabins hadn't been very comfortable with their drafty wooden walls and spiders scuttling about. She wondered if Mr. Ito would be able to grow bonsai in the mountains. He'd be so far away— at least a hundred miles—too far away to help her with the flowering quince. There were things she needed to know, now that spring was nearly here . . .

10

The Fourth Avenue streetcar rattled along its metal tracks. Sara sat squeezed against the window, next to a large woman in a scratchy coat with a baby on her lap. The baby smelled of sour milk and kicked Sara's leg in a steady rhythm.

"What wouldn't I give for a nice hot cup of tea!" the woman sighed. "I got soaked waiting for this streetcar!"

Sara smiled politely and edged her arm away from the baby's sticky hand. Its small fingers could pinch hard.

"What're you goin' to do downtown?" asked the woman.

"Oh . . . I'm . . . er . . . I'm meeting someone at the Orpheum," Sara said.

"What's playin' there this week?" The woman shifted the baby onto her other knee.

"I don't know . . . exactly . . . It's supposed to be a surprise," Sara said.

"That's nice. Wish someone would surprise me like that!" The woman lurched against Sara as the streetcar rounded a corner and then peered into her face.

"You're young to be goin' downtown all by yerself."

"Oh . . . I'm older than I look" Sara said. "Anyway, I've ridden this streetcar before."

She and Maggie had been to the Orpheum to see *How Green Was My Valley*. If she got off the streetcar at the big movie theater, she could walk the rest of the way down Granville to Powell. But she'd have to hurry. It was nearly three o'clock already. She stared out at the rain, hoping the woman would stop questioning her.

Aunt Jean had not suspected anything at breakfast. "Why do you have to come home so late?" she'd asked, transferring fluffy scrambled eggs onto Sara's plate. "I don't like you doing that. It still gets dark quite early."

"I'm working on a project," Sara had replied. It wasn't really a lie, but she'd crossed her fingers anyway.

"Well, I want you home before it gets dark," Aunt Jean had insisted. "That means five o'clock at the latest, young lady. I'll send Jamie to the streetcar to meet you."

"Oh, no! Really! I can walk home by myself."

Sara shivered and hugged herself tightly.They were passing False Creek, its still waters pebbled by the rain. Only a few more blocks to go.

Before she was expecting it, the ornate façade of the Orpheum Theater loomed ahead on the right. Sara jumped up.

"Excuse me," she said.

"Enjoy the movie," the large woman said.

"Thank you." Sara squeezed by. She thought she'd better cross over toward the movie theater in case the woman was watching. Carefully judging the traffic, she picked her moment and ran across. The streetcar whined away into the distance.

Sara looked up and down Granville. Everything looked different. The tall buildings seemed taller, stretching into the gray sky. The shop windows were full of haughty mannequins instead of bright Christmas displays. Even the traffic seemed different, honking its way bad-temperedly through the intersections. She looked this way and that for something familiar that would tell her she was in the right place. Keep calm, she told herself. Take a deep breath. That's what her mother always said in times of crisis.

"Are you lost, little girl?" An elderly man in a red uniform and gold-braided cap was standing beside her. "I've been watching you from the lobby." He gestured to the grand theater behind them.

"Oh, no!" Sara made herself smile. "I'm not lost . . . not at all. I'm . . . er . . . meeting someone."

"Oh?"

"Yes. We're going shopping . . . for a birthday present."

The man's suspicious look smoothed away. "That's always a nice errand. So . . . your friend has been delayed?"

"I suppose so." Sara began to relax. "I was just won-

dering . . . while I was standing here . . . Are we anywhere near Powell Street?"

"Powell's down a few blocks on the right. But you
don't want to go near Powell these days, miss."

"Oh, I wasn't going there. I just wondered where it
was, that's all."

The man nodded. "What time are you meeting your
friend?"

"About three. Oh!" Sara fixed her eyes on a woman
standing in front of a bookstore further down Granville.
"There she is. Thank you! Goodbye!" And before he could
ask anything else, she hurried away down the street,
trying to lose herself among the shoppers on the sidewalk.

Halfway down the block, she glanced behind her.
The man had gone back inside the theater. With a sigh
of relief, she headed for Powell. She must hurry. It was
getting late and she had to allow at least half an hour to
get home again.

Finally she turned from Granville onto Powell. It was
as if Saturday had become Sunday. Powell was empty.
Empty of traffic. Empty of people. Her footsteps rang off
the sidewalk as she passed little shops and restaurants
formerly bright with colored lights and paper lanterns.
Unexpectedly, she felt as if she were in alien territory,
an intruder who didn't belong and wasn't welcome. She
felt eyes watching her from shadowy interiors, but their
owners ducked out of sight as she went by. Her heart
began to hammer and she'd begun to wish she hadn't
come when she found herself in front of the Cho-Cho-

San Restaurant. Relieved, she ran up the narrow stairs to the Itos' apartment.

She rang the bell and waited, her heart beating hard. Silence. She waited some more, not wanting to ring again too soon and seem rude. Supposing she'd come all this way and they weren't home. She rang again.

This time, she heard the patter of small feet racing for the door and squeaks and giggles on the other side. Then the firmer steps of an adult and a low voice, sharp and scolding. The giggles hushed.

"Who is it?" The wary questioner was Helen Ito.

"Sara. Sara Warren." Silence. "Er . . . Mrs. Cameron's niece . . . I've come to see Mr. and Mrs. Ito."

"Sara Warren? . . . Oh! . . . My goodness!" A bolt on the other side slid back and the door swung open. Helen stood there, neat in her black skirt and white blouse. Three small children stared at Sara from behind her, their black eyes sparkling with curiosity.

"What are you doing here, Miss Sara?" Helen looked past her down the stairs to the street. "Where is your aunt? Who is with you?"

"Nobody. I came by myself." Sara was smiling widely. She'd done it. She'd got here quite safely all by herself.

"Nobody! Oh, my . . . Well . . . come in!" Helen smiled nervously. "Please. Come in." The children ran shouting ahead of them down the little hallway. "Please, Miss Sara . . . go ahead. My mother is in the parlor."

While Helen shooed the children into the back, Sara stepped into the parlor, then stopped in surprise. It had

79

changed since December. The window overlooking the street was covered with a piece of wood, darkening the room so much the ceiling light was on. One end of the room had been curtained off with a sheet. Cardboard cartons spilling over with dishes and clothes and pots and pans stood at the base of the wall, which had been stripped of its photographs. The furniture had been shifted around. Only the flag still stood in place in the corner, and the altar to Buddha, arranged carefully on top of the sideboard.

"Miss Sara! What you do here?" Mrs. Ito looked different, too. She wore a white kimono and her gray hair, always so neatly pulled into a bun on her neck, now fell loose and untidy far down her narrow back. She was sitting in a small overstuffed chair. It occurred to Sara that she'd never seen Mrs. Ito sitting before. She'd always been bustling around with cups of tea or pinning hems or holding up bolts of material to show them how it draped. "What matter, Sara-*chan*? You get lost from auntie?"

"No. I just decided to come and see you. I came by myself." Sara smiled, waiting for exclamations of wonder at her courage and independence. Instead, Helen and Mrs. Ito looked at each other nervously and then back at Sara.

Mrs. Ito said, "You alone, but auntie know you're here, yes?"

"No-o. I didn't tell anyone." Sara's spirits sank a little. "But it's all right, Mrs. Ito. My aunt won't worry. She thinks I'm at school."

"You lying to auntie?" Mrs. Ito looked very serious now.

Sara's face reddened. How could she explain? If she'd told Aunt Jean what she wanted to do, she'd have said no. She wouldn't even have brought her herself. Mrs. Ito and Helen didn't understand how everyone felt about the Japanese these days. If they could have seen the family around the table last night—Uncle Duncan planning the camps with such purpose, Mary looking so bitter and hard, Aunt Jean hurrying about, thinking only of keeping the family fed and Uncle Duncan in a good mood.

But Mrs. Ito's expression made her feel ashamed. "I just wanted to come and see you again, Mrs. Ito," she said. "And I miss Mr. Ito, and I need to ask him something about my bonsai quince." Tears pricked her eyes. "I didn't mean to do anything wrong."

"Well, well. Sit down, Sara. And give me your wet coat," Helen said soothingly. "We'll have you on your way home in a few minutes. But first I'll get us all some tea. I won't be long." She left the room.

Mrs. Ito patted Sara's knee. "We missing you, too, Sara-*chan*. Is difficult now see old friends. It shames us ask people to our so untidy rooms." She sank back into her chair and fell silent.

Sara sat quiet, too, listening to the comfortable clatter of cups in the kitchen and the sounds of the children playing in the back room. Mrs. Ito seemed lost in her own thoughts. After a while, the silence began to bother Sara and she tried to think of something to say. "You've changed this room around since I was here, Mrs. Ito."

"*Hai.*" Mrs. Ito sighed. "Everything change, Miss Sara."

Helen came in with a tray. "Henry's wife Iris and their children live here now," she said. "George's wife, too." She nodded at the sheets curtaining off the end of the room. "We've divided up the space as best we could."

She handed Sara her tea, and while Sara drank it, Helen talked about what had happened to them since Pearl Harbor. Her brother George had been arrested, taken away without a chance to even pack a suitcase, and his fishing boat had been confiscated by the government. Henry, too, was gone, sent to a road gang with the first batch of Japanese men, forcing his wife to sell their farm at a loss, because so many farms were on the market at the same time. "And we've had to hand in our radios and cameras, Sara. We had to sell my father's truck because we Japanese are not allowed to have cars anymore. And I was fired from my job." Angry tears choked Helen's voice. "We are treated like criminals! Worse than criminals, for they at least receive a trial and get a chance to prove their innocence!"

Mrs. Ito held up her hand. "Is enough, Helen. Sara-*chan* little girl. We not bother her with our troubles."

"I'm sorry, Miss Sara," Helen muttered. Her teacup rattled in its saucer.

"Don't be sorry!" Sara exclaimed. "It's not fair, what they've done to you! Where are George and Henry? Can they help?"

"No. There's nothing they can do. George has been interned in Ontario. And Henry is in northern Alberta. They're allowed to write but their letters are censored.

Henry is permitted to send home twenty dollars a month for his family to live on. But he's only paid twenty-five cents an hour. And it's too crowded here—it's difficult to live the way we like to live, in peace and harmony, in such a small space." Helen's face was strained and pale and she jumped in her chair as they heard a crash in the back room, followed by the wails of a child.

"You not worry, Helen," Mrs. Ito said. "Iris taking care of childrens." She gestured at the cartons. "Perhaps in camp we having more space." She smiled. "We packed now so we ready to go as soon as ordered. You see, we good citizens. We do what government say. Everyone seeing we good Canadians. Not making trouble."

"Oh, Mother!" Helen's voice was filled with affection and pride and pity.

"And maybe Mr. Ito can grow bonsai at the camp to make your place pretty," Sara said. "I thought he'd be here today—I forgot he'd be out at work. Could you tell him my quince is growing well and it even has some new little roots. I saw them."

Mrs. Ito began to rock back and forth in her chair. Sara stared.

"My father is gone," Helen said.

"Gone! On a road gang!" Sara was indignant. "He shouldn't have to do that. He was in the Great War. He got a medal!"

"No, Miss Sara. Not on a road gang. He is gone for good. We will not see him again."

"Not see . . .? Why? Where is he?"

"We . . . don't know. He said it would be better that way." Helen knelt in front of Sara, taking her hands gently. "My father's ancestors were samurai, great warriors who fought bravely in battle."

"Mr. Ito is brave. I know that. He saved my uncle's life."

"Yes. He served Canada with honor."

Sara glanced over at Mrs. Ito. She continued to rock to and fro. The silent rocking was sadder than Mary's tears.

"My mother grieves because he has gone from us, at least in this life," Helen said. "When the government ordered my father to prepare for transfer with the women and children to a camp in the mountains, he said he could not go. It would shame him to be prisoner in a camp. He has soldier's blood in his veins and soldiers do not give themselves up. He could not accept such dishonor. So he has gone."

"Is he hiding somewhere?" Sara hated the idea of gentle, dignified Mr. Ito, skulking in some alleyway, hiding in the shadows.

"He did not say. But we know he will not come back to us. He has said goodbye." Helen's face was sad. "He prepares to die."

"Die . . .?"

"That is why my mother wears white, the color of mourning." Helen's voice strengthened. "But my brothers' families are with us. We are here together. And when we go to the camp, we go together. And wherever we are, my father's spirit will be with us."

She'd never see Mr. Ito again. He'd never see the flowering quince. She looked at Mrs. Ito rocking in her chair, as widowed as Mary was by what had happened on December 7.

Helen took her cup. "We must run to the streetcar, Sara. You should get home before your aunt starts to worry. And, Sara. Do not lie to her anymore. She loves you and must answer to your parents for your safety."

Sara nodded. "I know." She stood in front of Mrs. Ito. "I won't ever forget you. And I'll write to you in the camp if you send me your address." She stooped and kissed the old woman. Her wrinkled cheek was soft as velvet.

Mrs. Ito took her hand. "It good you come, Sara-chan. We happy you loving us. *Sayonara*. Go with God."

Sara bowed. "Goodbye, Mrs. Ito. *Namu Amida Butsu*," she whispered. *"Namu Amida Butsu."*

Sara and Helen walked along Powell. At the end of the street, the traffic flooded Granville, the streetcars clanged, the people hurried homeward, the shop windows bright now, as evening began to fall.

When they got to the corner, Helen pulled her large-brimmed hat down over her face. "Hurry, Sara," she urged. "The Point Grey car is due." They got to the stop ahead of the streetcar and joined a small group of people waiting. Helen stood to one side in the shadow of the building behind them.

A woman in front of Sara said sharply to her friend, "What's a Jap doing out among decent people!" And her friend answered, "It shouldn't be allowed! But we'll be rid of them soon." She stared at Sara. "Some people aren't too choosy about the people they associate with!"

Sara felt her face go red, not for herself but for Helen. Helen stared at the ground, her hands gripping her purse, waiting for the streetcar to arrive before she would leave Sara alone, before she could escape back to her silent street.

It was nearly dark when Sara got off the streetcar and hurried toward home. Suddenly a dark form jumped out of the shadows ahead of her. It was Ernie.

"Ernie! You scared me half to death!"

"I meant to, Sara Warren. You may 'ave fooled yer auntie but you didn't fool me, matey. Where've you been?"

"I . . . I was at . . ."

"Don't try and tell me you was at school. I know better. I looked for you 'cos I was staying late meself."

Sara's heart sank. "Don't tell, Ernie!"

"Where were you, then?" Ernie pulled her under a street light and peered into her face. "Wot've you been up to?"

She didn't want to tell him. Ernie was against the Japanese. He wouldn't understand. But he was standing in her path and if she didn't get home quickly, she'd be in trouble with Aunt Jean.

"If you promise not to tell, I'll tell you."

"Cross me 'eart and 'ope to die!"

Sara told him.

"You mean to say you actually went to Powell, be'ind

enemy lines, like. You walked right into the middle of all them Japs all on yer own?" He shook his head. "Didn't you think you might be kidnapped and 'eld for ransom?" His eyes sparkled at the thought.

Sara shook her head. "They're not like that, Ernie."

"And Pearl 'Arbor didn't 'appen!" He stared at her. "You've got guts, Sara Warren." There was a gleam of respect in his eyes. "In fact—yer a bit of all right." He fell into step beside her. "Right you are, luv. Mum's the word."

11

 *April, 1942*

The buffety wind off the bay grew gentler and the constant cold rain gave way to soft warm showers. Every day, Sara studied her quince but it stayed bare—alive, beautiful, but bare of leaf or flower. Daffodils nodded beneath the apple trees. A parade of red tulips lined the garden path. And a sheen of golden green curved down the branches of the willow. But the bonsai quince was bare.

One day, Sara was walking up from the streetcar after school when she saw a familiar figure bent over the flower bed.

"Mr. Ito!" she cried. "Mr. Ito!" She ran stumbling and gasping up the hill. "Oh, Mr. Ito, I'm so glad . . ." She stopped. The face which turned was that of a stranger. "Oh . . . I . . . I thought . . . I'm sorry . . ." She backed away in embarrassment.

In the kitchen, Aunt Jean poured her a glass of milk.

"His name is Soo, Sara. We're very lucky to get him. It's terribly difficult to find gardeners these days." She sat down. "Now, honey, I know you like to watch but I don't want you bothering him. According to Mrs. Dunstan, he's quite temperamental and likes to do things his own way. If we interfere, he's likely to pick up and leave. There are people just waiting in line to grab him! And if that happened, I don't know what I'd do. Your uncle simply doesn't have time these days, with all this business down at Hastings Park, and the garden's too big for me to cope with by myself."

"What's Uncle Duncan doing at Hastings Park?"

"They're using the exhibition grounds there as a sort of collection area for all the local Japanese. Your uncle's been getting them all transferred in from their neighborhoods, seeing to accommodations, sanitation, food, sorting out who goes to which camp, organizing the trains. It's a big job. And, of course, that's all on top of his legal work. That's why we don't see much of him on weekends."

All that effort to get Mrs. Ito and her family and neighbors out of Vancouver. Sara tried to picture what it must be like for them at the exhibition grounds, all crammed in together with people they didn't even know.

"Where are the camps, Aunt Jean?"

"Well, dear, it's working out pretty well, because there are quite a few places scattered through the mountains where they can go—old mining camps, logging sites, migrant worker accommodations. In some places there are already usable buildings. In others they're being put up right now, good modern housing. Duncan says that, in some cases, they're superior to the homes being left behind."

"Do you know which towns they'll be in?"

"I know some of them. Your uncle has mentioned Greenwood . . . and Kaslo . . . New Denver. And I think he said Slocan City and Sandon . . . And there's a big farm at Tashme which the government has specially leased. We once spent a summer holiday camping all through there. It's really pretty and the mountain air is so healthy!"

"What do you think is going to happen to the Itos?"

Her aunt patted her hand. "I know you worry about them, Sara." She looked sad. "It's such a pity, what happened. Your uncle and Ito went back a long way together. War's a terrible thing." She got up to put the milk away. "But they'll be all right. I'm sure they'll be just fine."

Sara said nothing. Aunt Jean didn't know what had already happened to the Itos. She wouldn't want to know. She liked to look on the bright side.

"So don't bother him, will you, Sara?"

"Bother . . . ? Oh. Mr. Soo . . . No, I won't. Don't worry." Sara spread out her homework. "I thought all the Japanese men had been sent away."

"They have. Weeks ago. Only the old people and the mothers and children are left, and they'll be gone soon. Why? Oh. I see what you're getting at. Soo is Chinese, honey. Don't for heaven's sakes let him know you thought he was Japanese or we'll lose him for sure! Japan and China are old enemies. I'm sure he hates everything Japanese."

Sara sighed. Everything was so complicated. She should have paid closer attention to Ernie's lesson on the beach. Soo certainly looked Japanese. Suddenly, she caught her breath. What about the quince? Even though it was a Canadian quince, it looked Japanese. Supposing Mr. Soo found it? Sara grabbed her jacket.

"I'm going to take Fearless for a walk," she said.

"Fine. Stay away from the Point."

"I will. Come on, Fearless!" She headed out the back door, Fearless streaking past her.

Mr. Soo was at a safe distance, digging in the rock garden at the side of the house. Sara ran down the path and ducked into the shed. The new gardener had already established himself. His blue jacket hung on a nail and his bike leaned against the wall. He'd shifted the barrels of soil and fertilizer to a different spot and the flowerpots had been moved and were now stacked under the bench. Several flats of seedlings stood on the shelf at the end. But where was the quince? The windowsill was empty.

She peered under the bench and behind the barrels. It was gone. Anger rose inside her. He'd thrown away her quince without even asking! She flung herself out the door. Then she saw it, standing in the sun on the *engawa*, casting its elegant shadow on the toolshed wall. Sorry, Mr. Soo, she thought. I was wrong about you. But in the next moment she began worrying again. If Mr. Soo was going to keep the bonsai quince in plain sight, sooner or later Uncle Duncan would spot it.

She was going to have to do something. Her bonsai must live, and she would make it live. And bloom. Even bear fruit one day. It was all she had left of Mr. Ito.

Slipping the little earthen pot under her jacket, she let herself out of the garden onto the cliff path.

She knew where she was going. Last summer, scrambling up the Limey Path, she'd grabbed at a clump of sea grass to help her climb. As she'd pulled it down, she'd noticed a deep crevice gouged into the sand behind it. Now, as she slithered down the cliff, holding the quince close to her body, she pulled aside one clump after another as she tried to remember the exact place. Almost halfway down she found it—a long stretch over to her left—and pushed the quince gently back to the deepest part of the crevice, where it was sheltered from the wind. Once the sea grass sprang back, it was perfectly hidden. She'd have to bring it water every day. And she'd have to come in the mornings to pull it forward into the light and return after school to push it back again. It would be hard to do without being seen. She hugged her knees. Her quince was going to survive.

She got to her feet. Fearless was already at the bottom of the cliff, nosing around the scrubby bushes. She squinted into the lowering sun. A figure was running along Spanish Banks Beach. It looked like Ernie. She gave the sea grass one last protective pat and slid the rest of the way down the cliff.

She ran across Marine Drive. "Ernie! Ernie! Wait for me!"

He didn't turn.

"Ernie!"

He stumbled on, away from her, his head swinging strangely from side to side.

Something was wrong.

"Ernie, wait!" She sprinted along the sand. "Ernie! It's me! Sara!"

He stopped then, and turned. Even from a distance, she could see his face, white under the shock of dark hair. He stood still, unmoving, his thin shoulders drooping.

She stopped in front of him. "What is it, Ernie?" she whispered. "What's the matter?"

He shook his head, wordless, his eyes huge and black.

"Ernie, tell me." She touched his arm timidly. "What's happened?"

He reminded her of an injured bird she'd once seen in the garden, its bright eyes fixed, its beak slightly open, only its heart beating, beating—so wildly you could see the feathers move.

"Come on, Ernie. We're mates, remember? You can tell me."

He shook his head again. But this time a low groan forced itself from his throat and he sank to his knees in the sand. Sara sank with him, hanging on to his cold hand with her own.

"It's something awful, Ernie. Isn't it? What can I do?" she whispered. "Tell me what to do."

The words struggled out. "You can't . . . do nothink . . . It's . . . me . . . me mum."

"Your mum?"

"She's . . . dead. Oh, Sara. She's dead. Them ruddy Jerries killed 'er!"

"Oh, Ernie!"

"She's dead, Sara!" His voice rose, cracked, panicky. "I never thought . . . I mean to say, I was sort of ready for . . . for me dad . . . 'im being in the Commandos and all. But not me mum, Sara. Not me mum!" Ernie turned away, the tears running down his face. Ernie who never cried, not even when he'd broken his arm last summer. Now he cried—deep, rough sobs tearing out of his throat.

Sara hung on silently. There was nothing she could say. She thought of Ernie's mum, always smiling in the pictures he'd shown her, usually with her fingers held up in a cheeky V-for-Victory sign. She was fat and strong and cheerful. How could she be dead?

"She's been gone for weeks, Sara." His voice was full of horror. "Me and Mag, we wrote to 'er last week. We was writing to a dead person, Sara. A person all in pieces!" He gasped and his voice shook. "There was an air raid. She'd 'ave been in the shelter under the stairs. I can just see 'er sitting there with the Battler in 'er lap. She and that cat 'ad been through a lot of raids together . . ."

"It must've been a direct hit, Ernie. It must've been very quick."

Ernie stared stonily at Grouse Mountain. "They 'ad to get 'old of our dad before telling us. And 'e was out

94

in the desert—some place called Tobruk—and there was a battle going on, so they 'ad an 'ard job finding 'im. That's why it took so long to let us know. All this while . . . me and Mag, we've been thinking about 'er and talking about 'er . . ." His voice was bitter. "Them Jerries made proper fools out of us!"

Sara clung to his hand. Little shivers were running through him, one after another, like the waves curling onto the beach. Fearless whined, pushing his cold nose into their clasp, and wriggled his warm body between them. He was shivering, too.

Everything looked so peaceful, the water sparkling in the setting sun, the gulls bobbing in a little flotilla on the waves. Everything looked fine on the surface. But under the surface was there a Jap sub out there, watching them through its periscope? Everything looked safe but nothing was. Not really. David had thought himself safe on his parade ground. And Ernie's mum in her shelter under the stairs. Mr. Ito should have been safe after being so brave in the Great War. Maggie and Ernie were supposed to be safe in Canada. But the war had reached out its bony hand and hurt them all. And what about Mary, bitter and silent, and Mrs. Ito with her hair down her back? What about Mr. Lloyd with those sad hands? All over the world there were people weeping because of the war—Russian mothers and Italian wives and Japanese children.

Other thoughts hovered at the edge of her mind and she pushed them back. But they insisted, filling her head with pictures of her mother driving her ambulance through fire and pain and blood. And her father dodging the shell bursts blossoming in the night sky, his plane so tiny, the sky so big.

She buried her head against her knees trying to think of nothing and she and Ernie sat on in the gathering darkness while the ocean caressed the beach, saying "Ssh—ssh" like her mother's voice long ago.

12

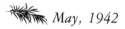 *May, 1942*

For the next few weeks, Sara and Jamie stayed close to Maggie and Ernie. It scared Sara to see them so forlorn, especially Ernie, who'd always been the brave one, pushing jauntily forward while quiet Maggie hung back. But now it was Maggie, always more accepting of what life handed her, who'd been able to accept her mother's death in that same stoic way. Ernie, who'd always been able to control any situation confronting him, was defeated for the first time and lost in a fog of misery.

One May Saturday, while the boys worked on the *Raider*, applying a fresh coat of paint for the summer's sailing, Sara got ready to tend the bonsai quince. Putting a little bottle of water in her pocket, she grabbed Fearless's leash and headed out the door. After watering the quince, she'd go up to the Lloyds' and find Maggie.

"Fearless!" she called.

Fearless loped across the lawn. Mr. Soo was close behind, waving a broom and screaming at the dog. Fearless was grinning, his stumpy tail wagging as he ran.

"Is bad doggee, missee!" yelled Mr. Soo. "Is digging big holes in my flower beds, missee!"

"I'm very sorry, Mr. Soo," Sara said. "Ba-ad dog, Fearless!" He wagged his tail at her.

"You keeping bad doggee out of my garden, missee!" Mr. Soo screamed. His little black eyes snapped. "Chinee peoples think doggee good to eat!" He brandished his broom.

It was hard not to laugh. "I'll make him be good, Mr. Soo. I promise! I'll take him for a walk right now! Come on, Fearless!"

Fearless bounded after her. It was strange. Fearless had never dug holes in Mr. Ito's garden. He'd always just lain contentedly nearby, watching Mr. Ito work. But he seemed to enjoy annoying Mr. Soo.

"Let's wear you out, Fearless." They ran together along the cliff walk. As they neared the Limey Path, they saw Maggie, sitting in the coarse grass at the top of the cliff. Her schoolbooks were spread out beside her, but they lay unopened while she stared out at the bay. Fearless bounded up to lick her cheek and she jumped, then smiled and hugged him to her.

" 'Ullo, you silly old dog," she said. " 'Ullo, Sara. Where are you two going?"

"To see you," Sara said, settling down beside her.

"I'm supposed to be doing me geography," Maggie said, "but I couldn't get started, some'ow."

"There should be a law against homework at weekends," Sara said. "What've you got to do?"

"Miss 'Unter 'as given us a 'uge blank map of British Columbia and we're supposed to fill in all the rivers and all the lakes and all the mountains and all the railroad lines and all the main towns . . ." Maggie opened her atlas with a sigh.

"I'll help you find things," Sara said. "Start with Vancouver and work your way east. There's English Bay . . ." She pointed to the coastal indentation on the map. "There's Howe Sound . . . and Mount Seymour, you can put that in . . ." She looked around. "And the Lions," she said, pointing to the twin peaks that rose behind the buildings of Vancouver. They were still tipped with snow, even this late in the spring.

"I like them mountains," Maggie said. "They look . . . peaceful, some'ow."

"Miss Ferguson taught us the Indian legend about them the other day," Sara said. "She's very keen on local Indian lore. She tells us a new story every day."

"Tell it to me."

"You want to hear it?"

"Yes."

"Well. It goes like this. The Indians call the peaks the Twin Sisters, not the Lions, and they're named after the daughters of the Tyee, or Great Chief, of the Capilano Indians who lived there long ago."

Sara stretched out comfortably on her stomach, gazing at the Twin Sisters. This was her favorite Indian legend.

"For many years, war had raged between the Capilanos and their neighboring tribes. There wasn't one family in the whole tribe which had not suffered hardship and grief and . . ." Sara glanced at Maggie. ". . . and . . . death."

Maggie nodded somberly. "Go on."

"Well, there came a time when the daughters of the Tyee reached womanhood and he decreed there should be a big potlatch—that's Indian for celebration—with lots of gifts and feasting and dancing. And he said to his daughters, 'Ask me for anything. This is one time in your lives when I can deny you nothing.' The sisters talked it over and they prayed for guidance, to make sure they asked for the right thing, and finally they knew what they wanted most of all. They went to their father, the Tyee, and they had to hold each other's hand for courage, because they knew what they wanted would make him angry.

"But they stood up straight in front of him and they said, 'O Father, O great Tyee, you have promised to grant our request and it is this. That you invite to this great potlatch all the tribes from the north and all the tribes from the south and all the tribes from the east and all the tribes from the west. And then we will feast together and dance together and war no more.' And their father, the great Tyee, was angry and he didn't want to do it, but he had given them his word so he had to grant what they asked. An invitation was sent out to the north and the south and the east and the west and all the neighboring tribes came to the potlatch, they trusting in the Tyee's honor not to attack them, he trusting in their honor not to attack him. And while they ate and drank and danced together, they forgot their hatred of one another and pledged new friendships. And by the end of the potlatch, they were no longer at war, and peace spread across the land."

"That's lovely," Maggie said softly.

"Wait. You haven't heard the end," Sara said. "The great god above them all was called the Sagalie Tyee. And he looked down upon the land and he saw what the daughters of the Tyee of the Capilanos had done. And he was pleased and said, 'Now that womanhood has come upon you, you have borne two children to your fellow man—Peace and Brotherhood. And so that you may be eternally remembered for this, I will make you immortal.' With that, the Sagalie Tyee turned the twin sisters into twin mountain peaks, strong and pure, which would stand side by side forever, as a sign of peace and brotherhood in the land of the Capilanos."

"Peace and brother'ood." Maggie sighed. "Not much of that around these days." A tear ran down her cheek. "This old world could do with a bit of that Indian magic."

Sara nodded. The two girls stared silently at the Twin Sisters, their crests gleaming in the afternoon sun. More tears were brimming in Maggie's eyes. Sara rolled over and sat up.

"Come on, Mag. Let's do some more of your map."

They pored over the atlas and Maggie filled in the rivers—the Fraser and the Thompson and the Columbia, and the mountain ranges—the Coastal, the Cariboo, the Monashee, the Rockies. They traced the CPR, the railroad line that they'd ridden west on their way to Vancouver from England. And the CNR, which ran a bit further north. They wrote in Harrison Lake and Okanagan Lake and the Arrow Lakes, both Upper and Lower.

They laughed over some of the place names.

"My favorite is Spuzzum!" said Maggie.

It was good to see her smile.

"How'd you like to live in Takakkaw Falls?" Sara pointed. "Nobody would ever spell that right! Oh, here's where I'd like to live—Stagleap. Isn't that a beautiful name!" She bent closer to the atlas. "Look! Here are Greenwood . . . and Slocan City . . . and here's New Denver."

"'Ave a 'eart, Sara! I can't put in every single tiny town!"

"I didn't mean you to put them in. I just . . . well, I heard their names a few weeks ago but I never knew exactly where they were."

Maggie looked at her curiously. "Is that where the Itos 'ave gone?"

"They're probably in one of those towns. I . . . I think Mrs. Ito might write to me . . . And then I'll know where they are . . ."

"Yer uncle might not like that," Maggie said. " 'E might not want a Jap writing to you."

"I know. But the Itos are different. They're good people. Almost like friends, Mag. I can't stop liking them all of a sudden just because they happened to be born in Japan. If Mrs. Ito writes to me, I'm going to write back. I don't care! They didn't have anything to do with killing David or bombing Pearl Harbor and it's not fair what's happened to them."

Maggie put her hand on Sara's arm. "Steady on, Sara. I know 'ow you feel." She gave Sara a little squeeze. "You're a good chum, Sara. You stick with yer mates."

"You and I . . . We'll always be mates, Maggie. And when the war's over and we all go home, you and Ernie and your dad will come and live near us in Peterstone and we'll all be friends forever."

"Let's 'ope so," Maggie whispered. "I don't know wot it's going to be like after the war, without our mum . . ." The tears, always just beneath the surface, began filling her eyes again.

"Maggie . . . how'd you like to know a secret?"

"Wot?" Maggie wiped her eyes.

"Down here." Sara got up and slithered down the Limey Path. Maggie scrambled after her.

"Look." Sara pulled the quince forward. It stood graceful as ever, the sea breeze shaking its branches gently. She pulled the bottle from her pocket and tipped the water out onto the soil in the little pot.

"Why've you got a plant 'idden all the way down 'ere?"

Sara told her what had happened to the bonsai quince. It was a relief to share the secret at last. And Maggie would never tell. "I'm sure it's alive, Maggie. Even though it doesn't have leaves yet, you can tell it's alive. It has a green look to it, don't you think. It isn't brown, the way it'd be if it was dead?"

"It's alive all right," Maggie said. "It's a slow bloomer, that's all. Not surprising with all that's 'appened to it."

Sara hugged Maggie. "I was afraid I was doing something wrong." She stood up. "Where's Fearless?" The dog was nowhere to be seen. "Here, Fearless! Here, Fearless!" She scanned the bushes up on the cliff walk and below at the base of the Limey Path. No Fearless. "I should've kept my eye on him. He probably got bored and wandered off." She began to feel nervous. "Where is that dog!"

"I see 'im." Maggie pointed. "'E's way down the other end of the beach. There—at the edge of the water."

"Look how far he's gone!" Sara was cross. It was getting late. "I'll have to go and get him. Do you want to come?"

"I can't. I'm baking gingerbread for dessert tonight. It's Ernie's favorite. Our mum used to bake gingerbread every Saturday night. I thought it might cheer 'im up a bit."

"Well, save a piece for me!" Sara said, beginning her scramble down the cliff. "I'll see you tomorrow at church."

She crossed Marine Drive and ran along the beach. The tide was out and the ridged hard sand of Spanish Banks rose from the water like a giant turtle's back. Far out at the water's edge, Fearless ran well ahead of her, chasing the sea gulls which strutted on the damp sand. They were teasing him, allowing him very close and then flying up, almost under his nose, only to land just a few yards further on.

"Fearless, come back!" she called. "Fearless! Bad dog! Come here!"

Fearless looked back for a moment, then with a flick of his tail, went on his merry way. If he just kept going, he'd catch up with one of those sea gulls sooner or later . . .

"Fearless, stop!" Sara ran on. "Fearless, you stupid dog! Wait till I catch you!"

Fearless paid no attention, enjoying the chase. And then suddenly he was out of sight round the headland.

Sara stopped to catch her breath and consider what to do. Maybe if she waited, Fearless would come back to see where she was. Minutes went by but he did not reappear. And then, as she gazed out over Spanish Banks, she saw the gleam of water running across the sand. The tide was on its way in. Her heart pounded. She knew how fast it moved at the Point. The sands would be covered in a matter of minutes.

She began to run. "Fearless! Come here! Come here!" As she went, the running got more difficult. The sand sucked at her shoes with a squelchy sound. She pushed the thought of quicksand out of her mind.

She rounded the Point. Fearless was nowhere to be seen. She glanced despairingly at the ocean racing in toward the cliffs. And then spotted Fearless halfway up the cliff face.

"Come down!" she called. "Fearless, come down *now*!"

He ignored her, facing away toward the cliff face, his stumpy tail erect as if he'd cornered something up there. But at least he was standing still. She'd have to go up and get him.

Slinging his leash around her neck, she began the climb. The cliffs were much steeper on this side of the Point and there was no Limey Path to make the climb easier. She clung to the clumps of tough grass and hauled herself upward, kicking toeholds, her feet slipping and slithering as the sand slid away under her shoes. Below, Spanish Banks Beach was vanishing beneath the incoming tide. Either she'd have to stay on the cliff until the tide went back out or she'd have to continue climbing and hope to find some extension of the cliff walk up at the top on which she could find her way home. Either way, she'd be late for supper and there'd be trouble.

Above her, Fearless was standing motionless on a narrow ledge. She edged closer, her legs aching, her hands cut from the sharp-edged grass. Finally, she reached the ledge and pulled herself onto it.

"Fearless, you wait till I get you home!" she gasped. "I'm never going to take you for a walk again!"

Her eyes widened. Fearless was standing in the mouth of a cave, staring bright-eyed into the darkness beyond.

13

The cave was hidden from below by the jut of the ledge. On either side of its rainbow-shaped entrance, two big rocks stood like sentries. Sara stared at them. They didn't belong here on the sandy cliff face. Someone had worked hard to haul them up from below. She crept carefully along the narrow ledge toward them, trying to ignore the sea below, now licking at the base of the cliff. The wind, so gentle down on the beach, was blowing hard on this side of the Point. It whipped her hair into her eyes and mouth and tugged at her dress. Using her fingers like claws, she clung to the cliff face and edged toward Fearless.

He was standing perfectly still, his nose snuffing the air in the cave for a clue to what was inside. She peered past him into the darkness but could see nothing. She put her arm around his solid warm body and felt it tremble. But he wasn't afraid. He stood steady as a rock, his tail high.

Holding onto Fearless, Sara dared to glance down. Now the waves were beating at the bottom of the cliff in steady rhythm. Over to the left, a little way out, a big rock protruded from the water. Around its base, the sea swirled this way and that, crashing against it insistently. Suddenly Sara realized where she was.

The rock out in the water must be the one the Indians called Homolsom, which marked the boundary between the Squamish and Fraser River tribes. No wonder the wind was so strong here. Miss Ferguson had said the Indians called Point Grey the Battleground of the West Wind. And the big rock, Homolsom, had once been some kind of minor god—the Tyee of the West Wind— who did bad things, like sinking canoes and tearing down trees, until he made the mistake of challenging the Sagalie Tyee himself. When that happened, the Sagalie Tyee turned him into a rock around which the west wind would constantly blow.

Sara grinned and hugged Fearless. "I'll bet nobody else in the whole school has ever seen Homolsom. That's worth getting stuck up here for!" The sand blew off the cliff face, stinging her eyes. "Come on, Fearless, let's get out of the wind." She turned back to the cave. "Maybe we'll find something Indian to take back to Miss Ferguson."

Inside, they stood for a moment to let their eyes adjust to the darkness. Then Sara looked around. The back of the cave was hidden in shadow. Here in the middle, the ceiling arched very close over her head. At the side of the cave, she'd have to stoop to avoid banging her forehead. It was very still away from the pull of the wind, which sighed and moaned through the grasses out on the ledge.

Something gleamed at her feet and she bent to pick it up. It was a black stone, polished smooth by the action of the sea. Excitement filled her. It didn't belong in the cave any more than the boulders by the opening. Some young brave must have brought the stone up years ago—maybe for barter, or for a present to his bride, maybe to decorate his clothing, or for some religious ceremony. The stone lay flat and cold and curiously heavy in the palm of her hand.

She bent to look for another, then stopped. There were a lot of the smooth black stones. They lay in a large and perfect circle on the floor of the cave, forming the boundary of what looked like a miniature sea. Except that the waves of this sea were made of silver sand, carefully brushed into swirling patterns in such perfect imitation of the water around Homolsom that she could almost hear them boom against the rock. Carefully, she set the stone back in place between its brothers so the sea would not spill out beyond its borders and stepped back, glad she hadn't destroyed this work of art by clumsily walking into it.

Her arms and legs ached from the climb up the cliff. She made for the shadows against the back wall and sat down. Pulling Fearless against her, she gazed out at the sky. It was getting dark and Aunt Jean would be wondering where she was, worried, maybe calling the Lloyds. But there was nothing she could do. She and Fearless would be stuck here at least another couple of hours unless she tried climbing the rest of the way up the cliff. But that would be dangerous in the gathering darkness. And if they by any chance managed to get all the way up without falling, they'd be lost in the thick pine woods at the top. Ernie had told her there were wild animals in those woods—bears, wolves. She was safer in the cave. But she couldn't help shivering and she pulled Fearless closer.

She was dozing when she felt a low growl rumble through Fearless. She snapped her eyes open, her skin prickling. Moonlight filled the cave. Fearless had jumped to his feet and stood stiff-legged in front of her.

"What is it, Fearless?" she whispered. "What is it, old boy?" He ignored her, concentrating on the cave opening. Sara shrank back as far as she could into the shadows. Now she could hear what had alerted him—a soft, scraping noise. Someone or something was climbing the cliff. She wanted to shut her eyes and not see what was coming. But this wasn't a scary movie. This was real. She waited, hardly breathing.

A dark figure blocked the cave entrance. It stood silhouetted against the fading light like some sea creature, water dripping from its long hair and beard. Then, with dragging step, it advanced into the cave and collapsed against the side wall. Raspy breathing echoed painfully in the cavern.

Sara kept perfectly still, hoping it would go away without discovering her, but Fearless broke free and ran across the cave.

The limp figure against the wall made a startled motion. "*Wah!*" Then, "You are sign promised by cave kami?"

14

Sara hardly dared believe what she was thinking. But in the dim light she could see Fearless's tail wagging ecstatically.

"*Hai, hai,*" the voice continued. "Good spirit. You have message?" Though thin and weak, the voice could only belong to one person.

"Mr. Ito?" she quavered. "Mr. Ito . . . is that you?"

The figure drew in his breath. "*Namu Amida Butsu!*" The prayer echoed faintly from the shadows. "You . . . ghost? Or . . . kami of cave? Come . . . where I can see you."

She crept forward, edging around the miniature sea.

He gestured feebly. "I . . . I thinking . . . I dream . . . Sara-*chan?*"

"It's me, Mr. Ito."

He leaned into the moonlight and she saw him fully

for the first time. His hair hung to his shoulders and his chin and neck were hidden by a thin gray beard. He wore white trousers, nothing else. His chest was sunken and shriveled, and just below the skin, his ribs showed, delicate as fish bones. He stretched out his hand, ivory in the moonlight.

"I thought you were dead," she whispered.

His eyes glowed deep in their sockets. "Soon . . . soon . . ." He was almost singing. "I wait . . . The Lord Buddha choose time."

"I . . . I've missed you so, Mr. Ito. Everything's different since you went away."

His sigh blended with the music of the wind outside. Backed by the wall, his stillness guarding his strength, he seemed a part of the place—the cave, the wind, the sea.

"Sit, Sara-*chan*."

She did, and Fearless stretched out comfortably beside them, as he used to in the garden. The cave wall behind her fitted, like her sitting-rock.

She'd held so much inside for so long. In the peace of the cave it all poured out. About Mary's bitterness and Uncle Duncan's fury and Ernie's mum. About her visit to Mrs. Ito and Helen. About the bonsai quince.

Behind his closed eyes he was not asleep. He was concentrating all his thoughts and energy on what she was saying, listening to her words and the feelings under her words the way nobody else ever did, absorbing her pain and bewilderment into himself. She finished and the sound of the sea murmured through the cave—hush, hush, hush.

After a time, Mr. Ito said, "Hurting will ease, Sara-*chan*. And quince will flower. Everything has moment. The Lord Buddha decide."

As it had always been, Mr. Ito said little but what he said contented her. They sat in comfortable silence.

Eventually, Sara asked, "What have you been doing here, Mr. Ito?"

"I waiting . . . I thinking . . . and praying . . . I bathing in sea each morning, each evening, to be pure when death come."

"The Indians bathed in the sea to be pure."

"*Hai*. Perhaps kami of cave ancient Indian, Sara-*chan*." His thin hands moved gracefully in his lap. "Indian . . . Buddhist . . . Shinto . . . Christian . . . men different in so many way. But men also same in many way. Same thing important to all—family . . . happiness . . . good . . . evil . . . life . . . death . . ."

There was a short silence.

"What happens after we die, Mr. Ito?"

"That depend how we live, Sara-*chan*."

"That's what our minister says. He says if we're good, we'll go to heaven . . . But what does that mean?"

"Ito thinking heaven just a word. Mean perfect happiness. But perfect happiness come in different ways to different peoples. You Christian, Sara-*chan*, all same my daughter Helen. So you and she and all Christian peoples do what Jesus teach, to live good lives. After dying, if you deserve, you go to God. To Christians to be with God is perfect happiness, is heaven."

"Do you think that's what's happened to David Lloyd? And Ernie's mum?"

"They good peoples. And Christian God is loving God who forgive small badnesses."

"Then . . . if they've gone to God . . . they're happy, aren't they? And Mary and Ernie and Uncle Duncan, they shouldn't be so sad."

"Is so. But they had no time for goodbye. Is hard to lose loved ones and face road of life without their company. So they sad for themselves. And grief take long time, show many face." He smiled at her. "Death is only a doorway, Sara-*chan*, and we all pass through. For some, the wait is short. For others, long . . ."

It sounded almost as if Mr. Ito believed in God, like she did. But he wasn't a Christian. And Mary had called the Japs heathens. Everyone knew heathens didn't go to heaven.

"Mr. Ito. What will happen to you, after you die?"

"Many road leading heaven, Sara-*chan*. Your God making peoples different, not all same. Why you think He make so, if He want only one kind peoples in heaven? Ito thinking, different peoples put in world to show different roads to heaven."

"But . . . you're a . . . a Buddhist. Do you believe in heaven?"

"Heaven, perfect happiness, something different to Buddhist peoples. Is not a place. Is called nirvana—in English, enlightenment."

"I don't know what enlightenment means."

"Means knowing whole truth about all things. To reach nirvana, Ito must also understand own self through and through. What is good, what is bad. Must learn what true good is and how he can be so good that truth and goodness fill him until no room left for bad. When Ito has discovered truth about all things, only then he reach nirvana. But nirvana not a place, Sara-*chan*. It a state of being. Is even possible reach nirvana while still alive. There can be no more perfect happiness for Buddhist peoples. The Lord Buddha help us with his teachings like Jesus help you. He ask us live good lives. Keep mind and body pure. Hurt no living thing."

"Is that why you became a Buddhist after the Great War?"

"*Hai*. In war men die too soon. Ito think is wrong shorten any man's life. Is bad karma." His smile glimmered in the darkness. "You not knowing what is karma. That our word for action which have effect. A man does what he does for many reason, some good, some bad."

"How do you mean, Mr. Ito?"

"Ito give example. Bad karma come from man wanting power and riches—that way war begin. But good karma come from man's thirst for wisdom and goodness—that way lead to nirvana. This thirst in man, this drive, this karma, strongest force there is, lives on even after death. When Ito die, his karma will in that moment be all good thing and all bad thing he did in life. But because journey to nirvana unfinished, karma must go on."

"I don't understand. What happens to it?"

He smiled again. "Your thirst for understanding, that

116

good karma. Buddhism say is hard for ordinary man learn all truth in one lifetime. He must listen, must practice, must be tested in good time, bad time. One lifespan not long enough. So when man die, he born again, to spend more time on road to nirvana."

"Born again?"

"*Hai*. The Lord Buddha is merciful."

"You can live over again?"

"Karma. Not body. Karma live on in different body, different life." He folded his hands. "So you see, Sara-*chan*, Ito not afraid leave this life. Karma go on to new life."

"I think you know everything already, Mr. Ito."

"Ah . . . not yet, I think. But if so, then I welcome death even more, knowing nirvana wait on other side of door." He laughed. "Ito may need many lives and many deaths."

Sara laughed, too. "I might never get there. I hate doing my homework!" Her smile faded. "And I told Aunt Jean a big lie."

"Tell her truth, Sara-*chan*. She may be angry but you deserve her anger. And you will feel good to have soul clean."

It was true. She hated having lied to Aunt Jean. And the fact that she'd got away with it made her feel even dirtier.

"I will, Mr. Ito." She smiled at him. "That'll help my karma."

"*Hai. Hai* . . ."

The moonlight had crept across the cave, tipping the

waves of Mr. Ito's little sea with silver. They almost seemed to move in time with the sea below.

Sara said, "I thought an Indian had made this little sea."

"I make as prayer."

"It's so beautiful."

"Everything beautiful, Sara-*chan*."

"Even snakes and spiders and mosquitoes?"

"*Hai*. Every thing beautiful. Each has reason to exist." He smiled. "Mosquito find other mosquito beautiful, yes? And fish know mosquito good to eat, so fish find mosquito beautiful, too, yes?"

"And the fish eats the mosquito . . . and I eat the fish . . . and the mosquito eats . . ."

"*Hai*. Your blood help mother mosquito lay her eggs."

"Ugh!"

"Is chain of life, Sara-*chan*. Every thing has purpose. Is your God not clever? Is not beautiful plan? And when you and I finish what we must do, according to plan, then we reach nirvana, each by our different road. That, too, is part of plan."

Sara gazed out the cave opening.

"What about the war, Mr. Ito. Why is war in the plan?"

"Perhaps to teach men how good peace is and to try harder for it. In perfect world with perfect men there be no war. But men not perfect. Men still on road."

"And that's why the Japanese, even though they're Buddhists, bombed Pearl Harbor and Hong Kong?"

"Not all Japanese Buddhist, Sara-*chan*. Some believe nothing. And some follow Shinto way, as I did when young, and believe death great honor if suffered for Divine Emperor. So some Japanese, of whom some may be Buddhists, bombed Pearl Harbor. And some Germans, of whom some may be Christian, are bombing Ernie's house. And some English, of whom some may be Christian, are bombing German peoples. Bad things come from bad things. War come from greed, and the Lord Buddha say enlightenment only come when men no more greedy for worldly things."

His voice was sad as the wind. He stirred. "Moon on floor say tide go out. Go back to auntie and uncle, Sara-*chan*. And love them very much, as they love you."

"I don't want to leave you, Mr. Ito."

"You must. Ito very . . ." His voice was fading. "Very tired now . . . Go, Sara-*chan*. Moon will show you way."

"I'll come back, Mr. Ito."

In the cold light flooding the cave, he sat like an ivory statue beside his silver sea. "Soon . . . Come soon . . ." the sighing voice said. "Is almost time . . ."

Outside the cave it was bright as day. Below, the wet sand was emerging from the sea. Carefully, Sara began the climb down. Fearless, his tail revolving wildly to help his balance, leaped sure as a goat from clump to clump of grass and reached the bottom first. His short, sharp barks encouraged her the rest of the way.

She looked back up the way she had come. The cliff

towered two hundred feet above her. There was no sign of the cave.

She felt suddenly cold. "Come on, Fearless," she said. "Let's go home." He raced ahead of her toward the Point, barking joyfully.

As she rounded the Point, she saw lights. They bobbed along the beach. They swung halfway up the cliff. They shone back and forth on the cliff walk above the Limey Path. She heard a voice shout, "I thought I heard a bark!" Then Uncle Duncan's voice—"It's Fearless! Thank God! She must be here—he wouldn't leave her!" And the lights spread along the beach toward her.

In another moment, she was in her uncle's arms, burrowing against his tweed jacket, smelling the good Uncle Duncan smell of leather and tobacco and shaving soap.

15

Sara sneezed for the fifth time in as many minutes and snuggled under the covers.

"I knew you'd catch a cold!" her aunt had said earlier, standing over her with a steaming cup of tea and lemon. "I said to myself Saturday, if that child doesn't catch a cold I'll eat my hat! Spending hours in a damp cave and missing her dinner!" Aunt Jean thought missing your dinner was the end of the world.

Sara wondered what Mr. Ito had been eating all this time. She'd once heard that the Japanese ate seaweed but she could hardly believe that.

She sighed. It was boring being sick and although she was still doing some sneezing, she felt much better today than she had on Sunday. Sitting in church, her head had felt like an overfilled balloon and fever had sent prickly waves of heat rolling through her body. Aunt Jean had put her to bed as soon as they got home.

But five days was enough. Her aunt had said, "Try to sleep, dear. It'll do you good." After five days in bed, Sara was all slept out. She stared at the crack in the ceiling. She counted the roses on the curtains. She listened to the sparrows fussing in the gutter. Then she pushed off the bedclothes impatiently. I can't stay here another minute, she thought. She pulled on her dressing gown and slippers and padded downstairs.

The house was empty.

"You're sure you'll be all right?" Aunt Jean had looked guilty. "I'll just be at Edna's, playing bridge. I'll leave the phone number on the hall table."

"I'll be fine, Aunt Jean. Really! Have a nice time!" She wasn't a baby anymore.

The slow tick of the living room clock echoed in the empty house. Another three hours before Jamie would be home from school. She turned into the kitchen. The canary, Trumpet, set his cage aswing trilling a greeting. She pushed her finger through the bars and he nibbled it gently. She poured some food into his dish, then roamed into the hall, looking for Fearless.

The mail was lying on the doormat and Fearless was stretched out on top of it, as bored as she was. As she approached, he opened an eye. His tail thumped the floor, swishing the letters in all directions. She stooped and gathered them up. Mrs. Duncan Cameron . . . Major and Mrs. Duncan Cameron . . . Miss Mary Cameron . . . Miss Sara Warren . . .

Sara turned her own letter over curiously. She didn't know the writing. She dumped the rest of the mail on the hall table and carried her letter into the kitchen, where she could sit at the table and read it comfortably. She tore open the envelope and found several closely written pages. Quickly, she looked at the last page to see who had written her. It was Helen Ito.

Dear Miss Sara,

You asked us to let you know which camp we went to and I'm writing to tell you. We are in Slocan City, which is a ghost town from the Gold Rush era. It is of course not a city anymore—in fact I would call it a dump—but we are trying to make it livable.

You might be interested in knowing what has happened since you saw us in March. Soon after, we were each issued a registration card with our photograph, fingerprints, height, weight, age, coloring and serial number. My mother, being issei, *or born in Japan, was given a pink card. We others, even the children, being of the next generations,* nisei *and* sansei, *and born in Canada, were given white ones.*

In April, we had to report to Hastings Park Livestock Exhibition Grounds. When we got there, we found each family had been assigned to a cattle stall. We were crowded, having Iris and her children and George's wife, Yuki, with us, but were pleased to be able to stay together. We hung up blankets to give us privacy from the people in the next stalls. There were almost two thousand people at Hastings Park when we were there. It was hard to keep clean. We used our little stove to boil water to wash ourselves and our clothes, but we felt ashamed to live in such conditions.

There were many children at Hastings Park, six hundred

from Strathcona School alone. We teachers and some of the mothers tried to continue their lessons, though of course we had no equipment. I teach here at Slocan City but need books and other things. The littler children enjoy being here. It is an adventure for them. But the bigger ones see little point in doing schoolwork as, being of Japanese background, they will not be permitted to go to college and they fear no one will employ them.

We came here on May 22. We sat a whole day on hard wicker seats in the train and when we got off, we were loaded on trucks to finish the journey. We were allowed to bring kitchen pots, a stove, a sewing machine, blankets, mattresses, clothing and enough food to last four days. It is good we did, because the camp was not finished when we arrived. Some families must live in tents.

We are luckier, as we were assigned to a shack, of which several rows have been built. Each shack has six rooms. In ours, the six rooms are occupied by seven families, which is not easy, since we are strangers, and we must share the kitchen and toilet. The kitchen has a wood-burning stove and we are learning to cook on it but it's difficult to judge the heat under the pots. The children gather wood every day to keep it going. All the families try hard to keep harmony in the Japanese way—hito ni mei-waku wo kakate wa ikenai—which means, "one must not make a nuisance of oneself to other people."

We have no bath in our building but must line up to use the communal bath. The water is often dirty when it gets to our turn. The struggle to keep clean is a matter of distress to us all, but especially to my mother, who has always been so fastidious. However, a stream from the mountains runs behind our shack and we bathe there if the day is warm enough. My mother finds it helpful to consider our difficulties character-building and says many times a day shikata-ga-nai, which means, "It can't be helped."

The Royal Canadian Mounted Police are in charge and Japanese World War I veterans help them run the camp. If my father had stayed with us, he would have been one of them. But he would have found no honor in such a position. We miss him very much but feel he did what was best. My mother prays to Buddha for patience and hopes to join my father in death before long.

My brother George is in Camp Schreiber in Ontario. It is good to know where he is and he is allowed to write to us. My brother Henry has heard rumors that an all-nisei battalion is being formed to fight against Germany and he is anxious to volunteer and prove his loyalty.

The mountains which surround us are very beautiful and covered with tall dark pines which smell sharp and clean. Our camp has no fence or barbed wire—there is no need—we cannot run away for we could not survive in the wilderness that surrounds us or ask help from the local people who fear and hate us. We are free to walk into Slocan City and shop, though the prices are high and we have little money. The townspeople are surprised when we speak English. I don't know what else they would expect from people who were born here just like them!

We can have visitors if they get a permit from the Mounties and we would welcome you and your family any time. We feel as sad about David Lloyd as you do. My mother sends her greetings and I do, too.

Sincerely,
Helen Ito

Sara read the letter twice, then sat back and looked around the kitchen. Trumpet chirruped in the sun-filled window. A bowl of fruit stood on the counter, ready for snacking. A fresh blueberry pie sat on the table and Aunt

Jean had a macaroni and cheese casserole on the stove, ready to pop in the oven when she came home.

Slowly, Sara folded Helen's letter into its envelope. The struggle the Itos were going through was a punishment that would last as long as the war lasted, a punishment they'd done nothing to deserve. She felt ashamed of what had been done to them. What would Mr. Ito say if he knew?

She went upstairs and got dressed. There'd be time to get to the cave and back before Aunt Jean came home.

On her way out, she saw her bookbag hanging by the door. She grabbed it and ran back to the kitchen, where she stuffed it with a couple of apples, a half loaf of bread and some raisin cookies. If Aunt Jean missed them at all, she'd think Jamie had had them. She called him the human vacuum cleaner.

"Come on, Fearless!" she called. They ran from the house.

Fragrance filled the garden. The pale drifts of apple blossom hummed with bees. Perhaps the quince . . .

She scrambled down the Limey Path and pulled her bonsai from behind the sheltering grass. Its soil was cool and damp to the touch. Maggie had kept her promise to water it while Sara was ill. Its supple branches nodded gracefully. But they were bare. She replaced it, pushing back the feeling of disappointment, and slithered the rest of the way down the cliff.

Sara and Fearless and the sea gulls had the beach to themselves. This time there'd be no trouble with the tide, which was still on its way out. But they'd have to hurry if they were to stay dry. Electricity filled the warm, heavy air and thunder muttered in the clouds over Grouse Mountain.

In a few minutes, they had turned the Point, leaping from rock to rock to avoid the suck of the sand, and headed up the cliff to the ledge. This side of the Point, the rising wind tore at her hair. Inky clouds towered up like monsters out of the sea, darkening the sky. She stopped, panting, at the entrance to the cave.

"Mr. Ito. It's Sara."

There was no answer. She glanced out toward Homolsom to see if he was bathing, but there was no one there. She hitched the bookbag up on her shoulder and ducked inside.

"Mr. Ito . . . Hello . . . I've brought you something to eat . . ."

She paused to let her eyes adjust to the gloom but quickly realized there was too little light coming in from the storm-black sky outside to be of any help. The cave was dark as night. She began inching her way blindly around the wall, her hands spread out on the cool rock to guide her. Halfway around, her foot touched something soft.

"Oh! Sorry!" She knelt quickly. He was there, asleep against the wall. "Hello, Mr. Ito." She touched his arm gently. She didn't want to startle him. "Mr. Ito . . . it's Sara . . . I've brought you something."

Fearless whined in the entrance.

"I've had a letter from Helen, Mr. Ito."

The sleeping figure did not stir.

Then she realized. She was too late. "O-oh." Mr. Ito's spirit had gone on its journey, his worn old body left behind like the chrysalis from which the bright butterfly has flown. Sorrow filled her for the things she'd never said to him. But she wasn't scared seeing him dead, the way she'd thought she'd be. And she couldn't be sad, knowing how he'd felt.

She sat in the dark beside him. Far out on the sand bar, the sea boomed in the rising wind and, as lightning flickered, thunder cracked like gunfire outside, and sudden rain slashed down like a silver wall across the cave mouth. Fearless, afraid of storms, ran to huddle close.

Did Buddhists have funerals? She didn't know. It seemed right to have a ceremony. She got out the apples and bread and cookies and, feeling for the circle of stones, placed them carefully inside, afloat in Mr. Ito's silver sea. Then she stood up and slowly said aloud what she'd learned in Sunday school:

> "For I was ahungered and ye gave me meat: I was thirsty and ye gave me drink: I was a stranger and ye took me in: Naked and ye clothed me: I was sick and ye visited me: I was in prison and ye came unto me . . . Verily I say unto you, Inasmuch as ye have done it unto one of the least of these my brethren, ye have done it unto me."

Her words echoed softly back from the darkness.

She felt comforted. Mr. Ito's spirit had found a new

home. He had been a good man and led a good life. Perhaps he had reached nirvana, despite his doubts. Perhaps at this minute, he knew it all, everything there was to know, just like the lesson the minister had read on Sunday.

"For now we see through a glass, darkly, but then, face to face: now I know in part, but then I shall know even as also I am known . . ."

It sounded as if St. Paul had known about enlightenment.

The rain slackened and she walked out onto the ledge. The air felt washed clean. It was time to go. The great boulders stood by the cave mouth like sentinels. Now she understood why they were there. But how could she move them? She pushed at one with all her weight. It rocked a little but stayed in place.

I need a lever, she thought. She searched the ledge. Nothing but pebbles and sand. She looked over the edge and, far below, spied a piece of driftwood bobbing at the base of Homolsom. Taking off her shoes, she clambered down the cliff and waded out into the pure cold water washing against the great rock. The driftwood nudged at her leg, offering itself. She caressed the rough cold surface of Homolsom, like the Indians of old who'd saluted it with their paddle blades to gain a favorable wind, then climbed back up the cliff with her prize.

Positioning the wood under the bottom of the boulder, she leaned hard on the other end and with a rocking motion tumbled it into the cave mouth. She took a last look inside.

"Goodbye, Mr. Ito," she whispered. *"Namu Amida Butsu!"*

The sun broke through the clouds and a shaft of sunlight arrowed into the cave through the narrowed entrance. She gasped. Caught in the sun rays, the *aiguro-matsu* rose from the middle of the silver sea, proud and imperious.

"Tree will tell you when you may touch it," Mr. Ito had said. Looking at it, she found herself nodding in obedience.

Slowly, she squeezed through the opening and walked into the little sea.

"Your *aiguro-matsu* will pass on," she whispered. "I promise you that, Mr. Ito."

Reverently, she picked up the ancient tree and placed it in her bookbag. It was lighter than she'd imagined. Squeezing back onto the ledge, she pushed the second boulder into place. The cave was sealed. The driftwood, its purpose served, curved gracefully back through the air into the waters around Homolsom.

16

 *June, 1942*

Sara and Maggie climbed from the beach after their swim and paused at the top of the Limey Path to catch their breath.

Sara said, "My copy of *Calling All Girls* came today."

"I'd like to read it," said Maggie. "Can I come over after supper? I'd come now but I want to write a letter."

"To your dad?"

"No . . . to Bob Jenkins." Maggie turned a little pink. "'E's one of John Lloyd's shipmates. 'E asked John if I'd be 'is penpal."

"Maggie!"

"Just doing me bit for the war effort." Maggie grinned. "But 'e's a bit of all right. 'E sent me a snap. And 'e wants me picture to put up over 'is bunk."

"Tra-la-la-la!" Sara sang the wedding march.

"Don't be soppy!" Maggie turned even pinker. "'E's miles older than me. And, anyway, I'll never get a chance to meet 'im. 'E's from some little town in Manitoba."

"Where's their ship now?"

"On the Murmansk run." Maggie looked serious. "It's freezing cold up there near Russia. And ever so dangerous. Mrs. Lloyd don't even want to talk about it, it's so dangerous."

Sara touched her friend's arm. "John'll be all right. Hey! Maybe he'll get leave and bring his friend Bob home!"

"That'll be the day!" Maggie laughed and turned toward her house. "See you later."

Sara ran along the cliff walk and up through the garden. Aunt Jean and Mrs. Lloyd were sitting on the lawn. They waved.

"How was your swim?" asked Mrs. Lloyd.

"Super! I wish summer could last all year!"

Aunt Jean smiled. "You look hot, honey. Have some lemonade."

Sara filled a big glass and drank thirstily. She loved the sweet-tart flavor. Her mother had said in her last letter that what she missed most of all because of the war were bananas and lemons.

"Anyway, Jean," Mrs. Lloyd continued. "Roger thought a change of scene might help snap him out of it. Now that school's out for the summer, I've asked my brother Bob if we can go and stay for a week or two . . ."

Sara knew who they were talking about. Grief takes a long time, she wanted to say. Shows many faces. But they'd wonder how she'd ever thought of such a thing. She put down her glass. "I'm going in to change."

She ran upstairs, almost colliding with Mary, coming out of her room.

"Whoa! Slow down!" Mary said. "I was just coming to look for you."

"You were?" Sara couldn't keep the surprise out of her voice. Half a year had gone by since Mary had sought her out. "Why? What's up?"

"I thought you might give me a hand with my hair."

"Sure." Sara tried to keep her voice casual. "What's the occasion?"

Mary's smile flickered uncertainly. "Jennie asked if I would give them a hand at the . . . servicemen's canteen. They really seem to need my help."

Sara ran into her room. "I'll just change!" she called over her shoulder. "Be right with you!"

A few minutes later, she was standing behind her cousin, the way she always used to. As she brushed Mary's silky hair, she couldn't help thinking about the last time, six months before.

"I've been practicing." She laughed shakily. "Your hair is going to turn out much better than it used to."

Mary's eyes met hers in the mirror. "I knew I could count on you, little sister," she said, and suddenly turned and hugged Sara. "Thanks," she said, her voice muffled against Sara's waist.

Almost all the curlers were in place when Aunt Jean came in and sat on the bed.

"Sara, Lorna Lloyd has had an idea," she said. "Her

brother, Bob Hale, is a widower with a little farm. She's decided to take Maggie and Ernie there for a holiday. She hasn't seen him since last year. Anyway, she wants to take you and Jamie along as well."

"Oh, Aunt Jean! I'd love to! Can we go?"

"Yes. I think it's a good idea all around. You haven't seen much of British Columbia up to now and Jamie will be good company for Ernie."

Sara twirled in excitement. "Super! Did you tell Jamie? When are we leaving?"

"Saturday."

"Oh, I can't wait! Where does he live?"

"It's a little place called Kokanee Creek. About two hundred miles from here. It sounds very nice. He has some horses and chickens and a couple of cows. It'll be fun, especially for city children like Maggie and Ernie." Aunt Jean got up. "We'll consider it settled, then. I'm going down to do the salad. When you've finished here, come and set the table, honey." She patted Sara's shoulder, then squeezed both girls in a hard embrace. "It's so good to see you girls . . . primping a bit," she said. "It cheers me up to see such fresh young faces . . . fills me with hope . . ."

"Oh, now, Mother." Mary gave her an affectionate hug. "Don't get all teary-eyed over us!" But her own eyes were wet.

Sara was putting the last glass of water on the table when she realized she had a problem. How could she go away for two weeks and leave the quince? It would dry out and die in the summer heat.

134

After supper, as she and Maggie settled down with their magazines, she broached the subject.

"What am I going to do, Maggie?" she asked. "I can't leave the quince."

"Wot about Mr. Soo?"

"No. I don't like him and the quince wouldn't either. Anyway, he might tell my uncle. No. I can't ask Mr. Soo."

"Well, then," Maggie said, "as far as I can see, the only thing to do is take it along."

"How can I?"

"Easy. It's very small. Take it in yer bookbag."

"I could, couldn't I. But . . . there's one other problem."

"Wot?"

"Well . . . There's another bonsai."

"Where?"

"In the same place. I've . . . been taking care of it lately for . . . someone."

"Well, take it along, too. I tell you wot—we'll each carry one, like a couple of bloomin' kangaroos!"

Saturday came. Very early, Sara and Maggie slipped down the Limey Path.

Maggie put the quince in her bookbag. "You've got the soil nice and wet," she said. "It should stand the trip okay. I'll be careful not to jog it." Her face changed as Sara drew out the *aiguro-matsu*. "Cor!" she breathed. "Look at that! Them roots ain't got no earth on them at all. 'Ow does it stay alive?"

"I don't know," Sara answered. "I pour water over the roots every now and then and that seems to be enough."

She didn't tell Maggie that she also said *Namu Amida Butsu* each time to make it feel at home.

"Whose is it?"

Sara paused. But Maggie had a right to know. "It belongs to the Itos," she said. "I'm taking care of it . . . till they come back." She couldn't tell her about Mr. Ito, not yet.

"It's a corker! But you'd better be sure yer uncle never lays 'is minces on it!"

"I know." Sara stood up, the *aiguro-matsu* a light but solid weight at the bottom of her bag. "We'd better go or they'll start looking for us. What time are you picking us up?"

"Nine-thirty. The train is at ten."

Late that night, the children tumbled sleepily out of Mr. Hale's car. Sara got a brief glimpse of tall pines black against the night sky, stars twinkling frostily through their branches, and then they were hustled indoors to cups of hot cocoa and bed.

In the morning, they woke to the slow jangle of cow bells.

"I love it already!" Sara said.

The girls hurried into their clothes in their little room under the eaves.

"I'm 'ungry as a bear!" Maggie said. "Let's see what's for breakfast."

Downstairs, the boys were already at the table in front of plates piled with pancakes and syrup.

"Flapjacks are my specialty!" Mr. Hale said in his booming voice. "Sit down, young ladies—another stack's coming right up!" He busied himself at the stove. "So, as I was saying, boys—and girls—do just whatever you like. Swim in the creek. Do the milking with me. Help yourselves to the hammock in the orchard. And ride, if you want. Those horses need exercise, with my boys off in the army. Ride 'em as much as you want. Good for 'em. They're getting fat and lazy!" His deep laugh rolled around the kitchen. "Just be sure to cool 'em off gradual on the way home and rub 'em down good when you bring 'em in."

They all four loved riding the horses. But Sara liked visiting them in their stalls best—the soft whicker of their welcome as she entered the warm, ripe-smelling barn, the muffled stamp of their hooves in the thick straw underfoot, the contented swish of their tails as they snuffled through their oats, the velvety tickle of their lips on her palm as they carefully accepted her offerings of apple and sugar. She owed them that, for each morning she stole some of their water for the two bonsai hidden in the tack room.

They learned how to care for the horses and control them and, before long, graduated from walking sedately around the courtyard to trotting, then cantering, around the field. When they weren't riding, they gathered warm eggs from under the skittish brown hens and helped Mr. Hale round up the cows. On warm nights, they lay under the stars, listening to the shivery call of owls whirring softly overhead. On cool nights, they played cards in front of the snapping fire or gathered around to listen to one of Mr. Hale's mountain stories.

Kokanee Creek tumbled almost out of control from the wooded hill that rose behind the little farm. It sparkled in the sun, bubbling and rushing over its stony bed. But when they paddled their feet in it, their ankles ached from cold in less than a minute.

"That creek's born in the high mountains not far from here," said Mr. Hale. "There's probably still snow up there, feeding this little stream." He clapped Ernie on the shoulder. "But fish don't pay no mind to the cold. Best trout in British Columbia come down that creek!"

Ernie shook his head when Mr. Hale brought out a fishing rod. "It don't seem right to kill somethink wot did me no 'arm," he said. "You go a'ead, Mr. 'Ale. I'll see to the 'orses." Ernie spent hours with the horses, silently brushing their tails and manes, currying their solid round bellies, scrubbed to a shine with stroke after stroke after stroke, his arm thrown over their strong backs, his flushed face pressed into their accepting flanks.

By week's end, Mr. Hale said they were expert enough to try a trail ride and led them in single file through the pines behind the house and over the hill into a stand of birch. They ambled along a sun-dappled path, the Kokanee chuckling and gurgling beside them. They rode silently, enjoying the soft clop of the horses' hooves and the pure high notes of the wood thrushes saluting them as they rode by. They stopped for lunch by a rough wooden bridge, munching thick beef sandwiches and spice cookies while the horses sipped delicately from the stream, then continued on their way.

"We'll hit the road into town in a bit," said Mr. Hale. "What do you say we stop in at Bob Maynard's place of business—get a soda, pass the time of day. Then we'd best start for home or Lorna will start worrying about her dinner!" His laugh boomed through the woods and bluejays flurried up through the trees.

Before long, they reached the road and turned the animals toward a group of frame buildings clustered on either side of a narrow valley.

As they rode into town, they passed a sign. It said— "Welcome to Slocan City."

17

"I've got to find a way into the camp, Maggie."

Sara flexed her aching hands, then bent back to work. Hugging the bucket between her knees, she pressed her head into the cow's warm flank, splaying her fingers around its velvety teats. Pretend you're playing a violin scale, Mr. Hale had advised. After a week's practice, she'd got the hang of milking but it still took her a good half hour against Mr. Hale's five minutes. Rippling the fingers of each hand in steady rhythm, she got the milk flowing again. It arced its singsong way into the bucket.

"I don't see 'ow." Maggie sat on a bale of hay, a basket of brown eggs on her knees, carefully wiping the straw off each one. "You said you 'ave to 'ave a permit."

"I'll get in some other way, then." Twisting her wrist, Sara aimed a stream of milk at one of the barn cats. He caught it expertly in his mouth. "I'm going to get the *aiguro-matsu* back to the Itos or bust! It was fate that made us bring it here, Maggie. Now it's got this far, I must take it the rest of the way!"

Maggie shook her head doubtfully. "'Ow are you going to do it, then?"

Sara frowned in thought, ducking her face to avoid the swish of the cow's tail. It caught in her hair gently, almost affectionately, as the cow shifted in her stanchion. "Whoa, Juno," she said. "Whoa, girl." How was she going to get into the Slocan City camp? As she worked the milk into the bucket, a plan formed in her mind.

"The camp's just the other side of town," she said. "And I know the Japanese are allowed into town, because Helen Ito said so in her letter."

"Are you going to give it to one of them?" asked Maggie.

"No," Sara said. "It's so beautiful they might keep it and never pass it on to Mrs. Ito. No. I must put it in her hands myself."

"'Ow?"

"Supposing we all rode to town the way we did the other day . . . and then I left you with the horses and joined up with a group of Japanese going back to the camp. I could just sneak in, in the middle of the crowd."

"Don't be daft. They've only got to look at you to see yer not a Jap!"

"Not if I'm in disguise." Sara stood up. "All done, Juno. Good girl!" She struggled with the bucket of milk to the barn doorway.

"Wot disguise?"

"I'll have to think of something. Do you think Ernie would help? He's always full of ideas."

"I dunno. 'E don't 'ave much get up and go these days. And 'e don't like Japs. I don't think 'e'll want to, Sara."

"Well, I've got to ask him. Jamie, too. I'll have to risk telling them about the bonsai. We haven't much time left—we'll be going home at the weekend—and I need all the help I can get to sneak that *aiguro-matsu* in."

Maggie nodded slowly. "Won't do no 'arm to ask 'im," she said. "It might buck 'im up—give 'im something to think about."

The boys were hoeing the vegetable garden.

"We've got to talk to you," Sara said.

"Okay." Jamie was only too glad to put his hoe down.

"We want to show you something in the barn."

Ernie didn't look up. "You go, Jamie," he said. "I'll stay 'ere for a while." He prodded the soil with his hoe.

"We want you, too, Ernie. It's important!" Sara pleaded. "I need your help with something. Please, Ernie. Be a chum!"

He sighed. "Keep yer 'air on. I'll come if you want." He followed them, dragging his hoe behind him. Sara led the way to the tack room and pulled the *aiguro-matsu* out of its hiding place.

The boys stared at it and Ernie pushed forward. "Blimey!" he breathed. "It looks two 'undred years old!"

"It probably is," Sara said.

"Whose is it?" Jamie asked.

Sara hesitated. Supposing Jamie told Uncle Duncan. But there was nothing Uncle Duncan could do to Mr. Ito now. She swallowed hard and launched into the whole story of Uncle Duncan and the bonsai and Mr. Ito and the *aiguro-matsu*. She finished by telling them what had finally happened in the cave.

Silence fell. Sunshine streamed through the window and dust motes floated in its beams around the *aiguro-matsu*. The lonely cave above Homolsom seemed unreal, a fairy tale place, and the ancient *aiguro-matsu* an alien refugee here among the soft-eyed cows and gentle horses and clucking hens.

"I've got to get it back to the Itos, don't you see? I promised Mr. Ito I would," Sara said. "Will you help me? I can't do it without you."

"That old tree's really been through it," Jamie said slowly.

"It has, Jamie, and it can't stop now. It's lived so long and it's come so far—this can't be the end of the road for it—not when the Itos are just a few miles away. We've got to take it to them. It has to go on to George, and then to his son."

"But it ain't right to 'elp Japs like that," Ernie objected. "That's giving aid and comfort to the enemy, that is."

"You know as well as I do the Itos aren't the enemy! Anyway, the *aiguro-matsu* has nothing to do with the stupid war."

"That's true, Ernie," Jamie said. "And remember the day we went aground at the Point. George Ito was the one who saved us. I vote we help."

Ernie frowned.

Sara held her breath.

Then he nodded slowly. "Right-oh. Let's 'ave a go."

"Thanks, mate," Sara said. They smiled at each other.

"Now, here's what I thought," Sara said. "I thought I could get into the camp by tagging along with a group of the Japanese returning from Slocan City. We could do it tomorrow. Mr. Hale and Mrs. Lloyd are driving in to Vernon to shop and they're stopping for lunch with the Bradshaws afterward. We could do it before they get back." She looked at Ernie. "What we've got to figure out is how I can get into the camp without being noticed. And I thought, with your dad being a commando and going behind the lines all the time, he might have given you a few tips."

"It ain't going to be easy," Ernie said. His frozen face was thawing out, coming alive. "Yer talking about going in in broad daylight, Sara. A daylight raid is no piece of cake!" He studied her face. "We're going to 'ave to change the old boat race a bit . . ."

"What boat race?" Jamie looked puzzled.

"'E means 'er face," Maggie said.

"We'll 'ave to do wot me old man did when 'e rode that bloomin' camel through Rommel's lines. Darken yer color a bit. And do somethink to yer minces. Give me some time to think about it."

144

After breakfast the next day, Mr. Hale and Mrs. Lloyd got ready to leave.

"We'll be home in time for supper," Mr. Hale said. "If you take the horses out, be sure to rub them down afterward." He climbed into the car.

"There are sandwiches in the icebox for your lunch," Mrs. Lloyd called from her seat. "Be good."

"We will," they chorused.

The car roared off down the road. The minute it was out of sight, they raced for the tack room.

Ernie had soaked some leaves and tree bark in water till it turned a pale brown. "Rub that on yer face," he commanded.

When she'd finished, he stood back and squinted at her. "Let me darken yer eyebrows," he said.

"What's that in your hand?" Sara asked suspiciously.

"It's a stick out of the wood stove," he said, working on her transformation. "Keep still or I'll poke you in the eye!" He stepped back. "That's not bad. But I can't do nothin' about yer blue minces. You'll 'ave to stay well away from the guard. And keep looking down as much as you can."

"What about my hair?" Sara asked.

"I thought of that," he said. "Yer going to 'ave to cover it up—like me dad did when 'e dressed as an Arab." He pulled a dish towel out of his pocket. "I borrowed this from the kitchen. You can put this on yer 'ead."

"A dish towel?"

"I seen Jap women wearing them out in the strawberry fields in Mission. Tie it at the back of yer 'ead and pull it down over yer fore'ead." His eyes gleamed. "Yes . . . like that. Yes, a dish towel will do the trick nicely."

"Are we ready?" breathed Sara.

"I reckon we are," said Ernie.

"Right, then. Let's go!"

Sara lifted the *aiguro-matsu* off the windowsill and placed it in her bookbag. *"Namu Amida Butsu!"* she muttered. "I hope the Lord Buddha gives us a hand today!"

Quickly they saddled up the horses and headed into the birch woods. They trotted in silence. The soft thud of hooves on the path matched the thud of Sara's heart. The bookbag with its precious burden rested lightly on the saddle in front of her.

Ernie, behind her, called softly, "All right, mate?"

"Thanks to you." She tried to grin back. But she was scared. This was no game.

They rode into Slocan City. As the others tied the horses to the railing outside Mr. Maynard's store, Sara slipped behind the building to wait for her chance. Mr. Maynard's big voice echoed through the wall.

"Back already?" He laughed. "My cream sodas must taste pretty special to bring you into town twice in one week! Sit down, kids, and rest yourselves. Try some of the wife's poundcake—fresh outta the oven—nothing like it, I can tell you!"

Lucky things, Sara thought. She loved poundcake. Maybe they'd think to save her some. She shifted the bookbag onto her other shoulder and then stiffened. A group of Japanese, carrying groceries, was straggling down the middle of the street, heading for the other end of town.

Sara swallowed hard, her mouth and throat dry. Her heart pounded. Suppose the Japanese challenged her? Suppose they said something in their own language and she couldn't reply? Suppose . . . They had passed by. She couldn't wait another moment. She had to make her move or miss her chance.

Taking a deep breath, she fell into step a few yards behind them, keeping her eyes down the way Ernie had told her. Ahead, the Japanese walked silently, looking neither right nor left, ignoring the hostile stares of the townspeople. She had joined them so quietly they hadn't even noticed her.

The town disappeared behind them. Now the pines grew thickly to the very edge of the road, seeming to threaten them as they went by. The sunlight glaring off the dusty road emphasized the blackness of the woods. The *aiguro-matsu* bumped lightly against Sara's hip and she put her hand protectively over the top of the bookbag. The people ahead of her had broken into conversation, now they'd left the town behind. They were still unaware of her silent presence at the back of the group.

After about fifteen minutes, the camp came into view. A man in uniform was standing in a hut by a wooden barrier across the road. Sara moved toward the outside of the group. The guard nodded carelessly as they passed him.

She'd done it. She was inside.

She paused, allowing the others to leave her behind. She hadn't expected the camp to be so big. She'd imagined a few frame cabins like her summer camp on Vancouver Island. Here at Slocan City, row after row of long, low buildings, each with a long black chimney sticking out of its tar paper roof, stretched into the distance. They looked like warehouses, separated from each other by a few yards of dirt, with nothing to distinguish one from another. Sara stared at them in dismay.

On either side of the camp, the mountains towered up, darkening the valley floor even on this sunny day. In the distance beyond the last building, she caught the cold gleam of green water—Slocan Lake. She shivered and wished she were back at Mr. Maynard's store, eating poundcake.

She began walking without any clear idea of where she was going, knowing only that if she stood still, she'd draw attention to herself. She marched along between the buildings, hoping she looked as if she had a destination in mind, praying she looked as if she belonged. Up one row and down another she went. Here and there, knots of teen-agers lounged against the doorways or squatted in the dirt, throwing dice. She passed some small children, chanting as they jumped through a skip rope. Outside one building, a line of people stood silently, each with a towel, inching forward as others emerged from a door at the far end of the building. Nobody paid any attention to her.

148

Just ahead, a woman bowed under the weight of two buckets of water turned into one of the shacks. Two children followed her, quarreling over a book.

"I want it!" cried the girl.

"You had it yesterday!" shouted the boy. "It's my turn!"

The woman turned wearily in the doorway. "Dorothy, let Shinobu have the book. He needs it for his homework." The boy grinned in triumph and wrestled the book out of his sister's hand.

Homework. Of course! That was the answer. Sara quickened her step, searching for a building that looked like a school. As she rounded a corner, a woman just ahead of her took a sudden turn to the left. Before she could stop herself, Sara had bumped into the woman and scattered the books she held onto the ground.

"I'm sorry," muttered Sara, keeping her eyes down. She bent to help pick up the books, ducking her head and praying the woman wouldn't look at her face.

"Oh, for heaven's sakes, look at that!" the woman cried. "Now the pages are creased! Oh, dear!" She clutched the books to her.

"I'm sorry," Sara said again.

"You should be more careful!" Distractedly, the woman rearranged the books in her arms, then looked directly at Sara. "Who are you?" Her puzzled gaze seemed to rest on Sara's face for minutes on end. "Oh . . . you must be one of the new ones . . . No need to be so shy, dear. We're all friends here."

Sara's face reddened. She kept her telltale blue eyes fixed on the ground. "Thank you," she mumbled. "Er . . . I'm looking for Miss Ito, the teacher . . ."

"She's marking papers in the schoolroom," the woman said. "I was just going in myself, to drop these books off."

Sara followed the woman into the building. It was dim inside and an oil lamp made a circle of yellow light on a rough table at the end of the room.

"Helen," called the woman. "Here are the books the Red Cross brought today." She dropped them on a nearby chair. "Oh, and here's a new girl, just arrived."

Helen Ito looked up in surprise. "I'm not expecting any new pupils."

"Well, you've got one." The woman waved and went out.

"It's me," Sara said, approaching the table. "It's Sara, Miss Ito."

"Sara who?" Helen Ito stared at her. Her eyes traveled over Sara's face and came to rest on her eyes. Recognition slowly spread across her face. "Sara . . . It's not Sara Warren? Good heavens!" She came around the table. "I didn't recognize you, Miss Sara. What on earth are you doing here, looking like that?"

"I came to see you," Sara said. "There's something I have to tell you . . . and something important I have to give you. Can you take me to Mrs. Ito?"

"Why . . . yes . . . of course." She turned out the lamp. "Come on. I never thought you'd really come, Miss Sara. How on earth did you get here?"

As they walked along the dusty street, Sara told Helen Ito where she was staying and how she'd entered the camp.

"So much for their wonderful security!" Helen laughed. "Here we are."

Sara followed her into one of the shacks. A long corridor stretched ahead of them the length of the building. It reminded Sara of the corridor on the train, with doors leading to different compartments opening off one side. They passed two of the doors. Behind one, Sara could hear small children playing. Behind the next, a bitter quarrel was going on. Helen gestured apologetically. "It's hard to live so close together," she said. "We get on each other's nerves. The smaller families have to share rooms with each other and it is hard to be forced into such intimacy. We Itos are luckier, being such a big family—we have a room to ourselves." She opened the third door.

Sara found herself in a dim room, shadowed by the mountains rising so close behind the camp. Seven narrow beds rimmed the room and beneath each one a cardboard carton held the occupant's belongings. A plain wooden chair stood next to each bed. Straw mats covered parts of the rough floor. A bouquet of grasses arranged in a bottle stood on a cotton runner in the center of a wooden table. It looked beautiful in its spartan surroundings.

The room was empty. "They'll be in the kitchen," Helen said. She led the way through a narrow door, calling out, "I have a surprise, Mamma-*san*!" She pulled Sara in behind her. "Look who has come to see us!"

The kitchen seemed full of people. Two women were working at the sink. Five children sat on the floor around a checkerboard. An elderly man sat in a chair in the corner, staring into space. Mrs. Ito and Iris and Yuki were sitting at the kitchen table, snapping beans into a black iron pot. Mrs. Ito looked more bent and frail than before. She peered at Sara and shook her head, muttering something in Japanese.

"Speak English, Mamma-*san*. It's Sara."

"Sara?" The old woman got up shakily and shuffled around the table. How different from the way she'd bustled about the apartment above the Cho-Cho-San Restaurant. "Sara-*chan*?" She frowned in puzzlement. "Is Sara-*chan*?"

Sara laughed. "Ernie disguised me so I could get past the guard."

"Sara-*chan*! . . . Oh! I so happy seeing you here! Come . . . Come . . . sit at table. You see now we and our neighbors, Yamashita family, prepare supper." She waved Sara to a chair with something of her old, fluttery hospitality. "Quick, Iris . . . quick, we making tea for Miss Sara."

Iris ran to the wood stove at the base of the black chimney pipe and pushed in a handful of kindling. Flames flared and crackled inside and Iris encouraged them, poking more wood through the iron door. Filling a kettle from the bucket on the floor, she set it on top to boil.

The Ito children gathered close to Sara, leaning against her knee, black eyes fixed on her face. The women at the sink abandoned what they were doing and helped the old man out of his chair. Shooing their own children before them, they left the kitchen, smiling and bowing as they went and saying, in high, fluting voices, *"Hito ni meiwaku wo kakate wa ikenai."*

"Miss Sara has come to bring us something, Mama-*san,*" Helen said. "She hasn't much time. Her friends are waiting in town. So begin, Sara. Tell us why you came."

Mary's thin, high scream re-echoed in her head. She looked down at her hands. They lay in her lap, upturned and fingerwide. She looked up at their faces, wreathed in smiles, expectant, trusting.

Slowly, she told her story, starting with the day Fearless ran away from her at the beach and ending with the sealing of the cave above Homolsom. The children pressed against her uncomprehendingly while Iris and Yuki wept quietly into their handkerchiefs. Helen turned abruptly toward the stove and filled the teapot, then took cups and saucers from a shelf and brought them rattling to the table.

Sara raised her eyes fearfully to Mrs. Ito.

"Ah . . ." Tears ran down the old woman's face as she rocked back and forth in her chair. "You brave girl, Sara-*chan.* The Lord Buddha blessing you today." She smiled at Sara. "Now I know husband on way he wished to go." She clasped Sara's hands in her own. "You good friend, Sara-*chan.*"

"I brought you something from him," Sara said. Carefully, she opened her bookbag and set the *aiguro-matsu* on the table.

"*Wah*!" Everyone breathed in awe. "Ah! . . . Ah!"

They circled the ancient tree. It glowed in the simple room, its pine needles gleaming like dark green silk, the seamed bark of its broad trunk the brown of finest leather.

Relief filled Sara. It was done. She had the sudden sense that Mr. Ito himself was present, that for this moment they were all together again.

A heavy knock on the outer door broke the spell.

"I'll go," Yuki said.

There was a murmur of voices out in the corridor and footsteps approached the kitchen. Yuki reentered the room.

She was followed by Uncle Duncan.

18

There was nowhere to hide. Uncle Duncan blocked the doorway. Filled the room. Breathed up all the air.

"Good day," He bowed formally. "I'm here on a tour of inspection at the request of the Red Cross." He looked around the kitchen. "Is everything satisfactory? Is there anything essential that is not being provided for you?"

Mrs. Ito started shakily toward him. Her daughters hurried to support her. "Major Cameron . . . is you?"

His official manner dissolved into a look of puzzlement. "How do . . . ?" He stared at her. "Mrs. . . . . Ito?"

"You coming visit Mrs. Ito one more time?" The old woman peered up into his face. "*Wah*, Major-*san*. If only Ito seeing our families together again . . . I so happy you here!"

Uncle Duncan looked embarrassed.

Helen Ito said curtly, "The Major is here on business, Mother."

"Well . . . yes, that's true . . . I am," said Uncle Duncan. He gestured at the bare room. "But I . . . I'm very sorry to see you living like this . . . I really had no idea that conditions were so . . ." His voice trailed off.

Sara fixed her eyes on the floor and edged as far as she could behind Yuki. Pain spread across her shoulders, and she realized she was holding her breath. She let it out carefully through her closed lips.

Mrs. Ito was smiling up into Uncle Duncan's face. "It most happy day in long time, Major-*san* . . . seeing you . . . seeing Miss Sara . . ."

Thick silence filled the room. Time seemed to have stopped and they stood frozen into a staged tableau— Yuki and Iris and Helen by the table, Mrs. Ito clinging to Uncle Duncan's arm—even the children were still.

A fly buzzed frantically against the windowpane.

"Miss Sara?" Uncle Duncan frowned. "I don't understand."

"She coming see us, too." Mrs. Ito smiled happily at Sara. "Is good harmony here today."

Uncle Duncan stared across the room.

Sara's heart was falling, falling—plunging down through her body. Hot color flooded her face, then drained away. Her uncle was coming toward her. She tried to turn her telltale eyes aside. The room began whirling like the fly at the window, turning, turning, till she felt giddy and sick, becoming smaller and smaller, a tiny windmill, a golden point in her brain. The buzzing in the window grew to a roar that filled her ears. And then she and the roar and the golden point melted and sank into darkness.

Cool lake air touched her cheek. Voices murmured on either side, rising, falling. Was she moving or were they? Safe in her dark world, she did not want to open her eyes. The scent of pines reached her nostrils, combined with something more familiar. She was bumping gently against a rough jacket from which rose the faint fragrance of pipe tobacco.

Helen Ito's voice said, "She's a good girl, Major Cameron. She meant no harm by coming here. If you only knew what she's been through . . ."

Her uncle's voice rumbled against her ear. "I'm just beginning to realize, Helen. I've been too preoccupied with my own concerns. The war has done terrible things to all of us, Helen. But I'm going to take her home and get everything straightened out. And I'll see what I can do to make things better for all of you here at Slocan City."

"We're doing our best, Major," Helen said. "We are anxious to show *enryo*—restraint—and demonstrate we are loyal Canadians willing to do whatever the government wants. But for our obedience we have been rewarded with separated families and confiscated property. Our past is in ruins. Our present is in limbo. As for our future . . ." Her voice shook. "Aren't we fighting a war against lawlessness, Major? Well, what kind of British law says you can do this to thousands of good law-abiding people without benefit of trial or proof of guilt?"

"I'm so sorry, Helen. So sorry . . . It's the war. Pearl Harbor took us by surprise. We feared invasion . . . There was no time to think things out or separate the innocent from the guilty . . . It was a question of defense against sabotage . . ."

"Sabotage. By old women and babies. What a terrible enemy!"

"I know." He cleared his throat. "The war in the Pacific seems to be going better since our victory at Midway. Perhaps, as the situation eases, we'll be able to get you all back to your homes . . ."

"I won't hold my breath." Helen's voice was bitter.

"We'll keep in touch, Helen. Young Sara had the right idea."

A car door opened and Sara was placed inside, a blanket tucked around her. Her uncle's hands were gentle. It was safe to open her eyes.

19

They sat in church together, the scent of roses wafting through the open windows. The Reverend Mr. Colthorpe climbed into the pulpit and Sara glanced down the pew and grinned. Uncle Duncan's chin had dropped onto his chest, right on cue.

"Judge not that ye be not judged." Mr. Colthorpe warmed to his theme. "For with what judgment ye judge ye shall be judged and with what measure ye mete it shall be measured to you again . . ."

Do as you would be done by, her mother had always said. Maybe that was the way to peace. If the Germans and the Japanese had done as they would be done by, maybe the world wouldn't be all upside down.

Her thoughts turned to Mr. Ito. She'd taken Uncle Duncan to the place above Homolsom so their two spirits could make peace on the lonely ledge. Where was Mr. Ito's spirit now? Far along on the next stage of his journey? There were times she was sure she heard his voice, sighing on the wind, murmuring at the sea's edge, promising understanding and peace some far-off day when men had gone a little further on their road to enlightenment.

"Let not your heart be troubled!" cried Mr. Colthorpe. "Ye believe in God, believe also in me. In my Father's house are many mansions: if it were not so I would have told you. I go to prepare a place for you. And if I go and prepare a place for you I will come again and receive you unto myself: that where I am, there ye may be also . . ."

Many mansions . . .

On the way home, a question nagged at the edge of Sara's mind. "Uncle Duncan, you're a word expert. What does it mean, 'In my Father's house are many mansions'? How can many mansions be inside one house? It's like a riddle. It doesn't make sense." She frowned. "And yet . . . it's funny . . . but when Mr. Colthorpe said that bit, even though it didn't make sense, it made me feel so peaceful . . ."

"So it should, Sara." He turned the Buick onto Alma. "But I like your questioning mind. You're right. The sentence as it stands makes no sense at all. And that's because, hundreds of years ago, a mistake was made by one of the scholars who was translating St. John's Gospel from its original Greek into English. The original Greek word used was *manse*. But this scholar didn't know the

English meaning of *manse* and for some reason didn't bother to ask anyone else. Perhaps—being human—he was ashamed of his ignorance, didn't want to admit it. Anyway, whatever the reason, he put down what he thought it sounded most like—the English word *mansion*. And it has stayed that way ever since. Because, even though it doesn't make sense, the words still give comfort, which was the original intention."

"Do you know what *manse* really means?"

"Well, now . . . if I remember my ancient Greek correctly, it can have a variety of meanings. But, mainly, it means 'provided for' or 'provision for.' I think what the writer must have meant to convey was a sense that in God's house, there is provision for many, not just a special few."

So there it was, right in the Bible. Heaven was there for everyone. God would provide for Mr. Ito.

"Speaking of father's houses," Mary said, "there's going to be a bit more room at my father's house, Sara."

"What do you mean?"

"I told Mum and Dad last night. Jennie and Caro and I are going to share an apartment in town. I'll be moving out soon . . . and I've been wondering what to do with my canopy bed . . ."

"Oh, Mary!"

They were still laughing when the Buick turned into the driveway.

"I'm going up to water the quince," Sara said.

"Fine, honey," Aunt Jean said. "Mary, come and give

me a hand with lunch. I've got a good one today, to celebrate Jamie and Sara's homecoming."

Homecoming. She must put that in her list of favorite words. Could it be one of the meanings of *manse?*

The quince stood on her windowsill where it could feel the breeze off English Bay. In the three days since their return from Kokanee Creek, several leaves had uncurled along its branches and there was a flower, five frilled white petals tinged with a tracery of pink, like the veins under a baby's skin. She bent and studied the circle of delicate gold-tipped stamens rising from its center like a fairy crown. Faint fragrance filled the air around it.

"How's it doing?" her uncle said from the doorway.

"Come and see."

"You've done a good job with it, Sara," he said. "Mr. Ito would be proud of you."

"I wish he could see it." She gently touched the moss at its base.

"I'm sorry for what happened."

"He understood."

Together they looked across at Grouse Mountain. He put his arm around her shoulder. "These are historic times, Sara. Your children will study this war in their history books. They'll learn all about the evacuation of Dunkirk and the battles of Britain and Tobruk and Midway." He smiled down at her. "Perhaps you'll write a book of your own one day."

She nodded. "Perhaps." But she knew that if she ever wrote a book about the war, it would be about Mary's scream and Mr. Lloyd's hands and Uncle Duncan's face in the cold moonlight. About Ernie's grief and Helen's bitterness. And Mr. Ito and his bonsai tree.